Kelly could feel the breath catch in her throat as his lips brushed the curve of her ear.

"I can feel you tremble in my arms," Nick said. "You want me, sweetheart, and God knows I've been in a fever for you since you barged into my apartment yesterday afternoon." His lips caressed the nape of her neck and brushed light, teasing kisses beneath the sunstreaked ringlets of her hair.

"I love these bouncy little curls of yours," he whispered, burying his lips in her hair. "Your hair is like a silky golden fleece. I bet those curls would wind themselves around my finger and cling like a lover's embrace. Would they do that, Kelly?"

"Yes," she gasped, feeling as if her bones were melting. "No!" She shook her head. "I don't know. I wish you'd stop that."

"You don't like it?" he asked. "I guess I'll have to find something you do like, sweetheart." Suddenly he stepped back and turned her into his embrace, his arms binding her soft curves to his lean, hard body. "I like this better, too," he said hoarsely. "God, you're so soft and sweet against me. See how beautifully you fit into my arms?"

She did see, she thought dreamily. It seemed so unbelievably right to be so close to him.

WHAT ARE *LOVESWEPT* ROMANCES?

They are stories of true romance and touching emotion. We believe those two very important ingredients are constants in our highly sensual and very believable stories in the *LOVESWEPT* line. Our goal is to give you, the reader, stories of consistently high quality that may sometimes make you laugh, sometimes make you cry, but are always fresh and creative and contain many delightful surprises within their pages.

Most romance fans read an enormous number of books. Those they truly love, they keep. Others may be traded with friends and soon forgotten. We hope that each *LOVESWEPT* romance will be a treasure—a "keeper." We will always try to publish

LOVE STORIES YOU'LL NEVER FORGET
BY AUTHORS YOU'LL ALWAYS REMEMBER

The Editors

LOVESWEPT · 27

Iris Johansen
The Bronzed Hawk

BANTAM BOOKS · TORONTO · NEW YORK · LONDON · SYDNEY

THE BRONZED HAWK

A Bantam Book / December 1983

*LOVESWEPT and the wave device are trademarks of
Bantam Books, Inc.*

ISBN 0-553-21632-5

Published simultaneously in the United States and Canada

*Bantam Books are published by Bantam Books, Inc. Its
trademark, consisting of the words "Bantam Books" and the
portrayal of a rooster, is Registered in U.S. Patent and Trademark Office and in other countries. Marca Registrada. Bantam
Books, Inc., 666 Fifth Avenue, New York, New York 10103.*

PRINTED IN THE UNITED STATES OF AMERICA

O   0 9 8 7 6 5 4 3 2 1

One

"I'm sorry, Miss McKenna, but Mr. O'Brien refuses to see you." The security guard at the desk in the lobby of the high-rise apartment building returned the phone to its cradle. There was a trace of genuine regret in his face as he regarded the disappointed expression of the young woman across from him.

Kelly bit her lower lip, and her jade green eyes darkened to almost emerald. She hadn't really expected any other answer than the one transmitted to her by the guard, but she had admitted to a hope that O'Brien would miraculously change his mind and see her. Her lips curved in a wry smile. What a miracle that would have been! Nick O'Brien's antipathy toward journalists and the media was practically legend. He had been refusing both her written requests for an interview and all her phone calls for over three weeks now. She sighed. She hadn't wanted to use the wild card that might gain her entrance to his presence, but now it seemed that she had no choice.

She reached into her voluminous bone leather shoulder bag, drew out a long white business envelope, and handed it to the burly, gray-haired security guard. Her glowingly appealing smile was the same one that once had gotten her past the bodyguard of a South American dictator. And the article resulting from that had earned a Pulitzer Prize nomination. The memory made her feel even more confident . . . and bold. "I wonder if you could possibly give this to Mr. O'Brien for me," she pleaded softly. Her wide-set jade green eyes in their extravagant frame of dark lashes were brimming with a distress that was only half feigned. "I'm sure there must be some mistake. If you'll just give him this envelope, I'm positive that everything will be straightened out in no time."

The security guard shook his head doubtfully. "I don't know, Miss McKenna," he said uneasily. "I'm not supposed to leave my desk without a replacement. The building manager would have my job if he happened to drop by and I wasn't on duty." Despite his protests, his face softened infinitesimally as he gazed at the young woman before him. There was something very appealing about Kelly McKenna. She had an aura of breathless, wide-eyed eagerness, as if just living was a vividly exciting adventure.

Her ash blond hair was now sun-streaked to almost white gold in places. It was cut so that it clustered about her face, ears, and the nape of her neck in a riot of silken, glossy curls that tempted a man to wrap the strands around his fingers. The most arresting feature of her thin face were her magnificent green eyes. Her lips were well defined and had a curve that was sweetly memorable. She had a vaguely fragile air about her that was belied by her golden tan and the determined tilt of her chin.

That chin was squared now as Kelly McKenna said persuasively, "I'll be glad to fill in for you until you get back. It will only take you a moment, and I can handle anything that comes along. I earned my black belt in karate last summer."

The security guard disguised a chuckle as a cough. Kelly McKenna couldn't be more than an inch or two over five feet tall and except for her height, she looked like a fashion model. Her designer blouse was left open stylishly to display just a hint of cleavage; her rust suede skirt was slit to the thigh in front to reveal tantalizing glimpses of shapely limbs, emphasized by knee-length high-heeled boots. She looked about as lethal as a baby fresh from its evening bath.

He took the envelope and rose slowly. "In that case I'll feel safe to leave you in charge," he said solemnly, his eyes twinkling. "You watch sharp now." He moved briskly to the elevator and pressed the button for the penthouse, leaving Kelly to stare after him with satisfaction mixed with a tinge of displeasure.

It certainly wasn't the first time she had encountered indulgent condescension from the male sex, she thought crossly, but still it never failed to irritate her. She was well aware that her size and general air of fragile femininity were deceptive, but it took a good deal of effort to convince men of that! Most of the time she found it wasn't worth the effort and saved her strength for the more important battles that faced a woman photo-journalist in a field dominated by men. When she was first starting out, she'd thought her "image" was very important and, trying to look anything but delicate and feminine, she'd chosen a wardrobe of only pantsuits and jeans. But she soon found that she was defeating her purpose. The day she had overheard herself described as "cute and cuddly" in a pair of shapeless bib overalls, she'd grimly abandoned that fruitless strategy.

This afternoon she was wearing the most sophisticated outfit in her entire wardrobe; even *it* hadn't caused the security guard to treat her with respect for her maturity, she mused. It certainly didn't bode well for her coming confrontation with Nick O'Brien, who was a much more dangerous proposition. She had done extensive, in-depth research on O'Brien before approaching him for this interview. What she had learned would have intimidated her under normal circumstances . . . if only it weren't for that blasted bet she'd made with her editor, Mac Devlin!

Then she chuckled and shook her head ruefully. She wasn't being honest with herself. The more difficult or dangerous an assignment, the more she enjoyed it, and Mac had known that when he'd made that damned bet with her. She was well aware that Devlin was manipulating her, but the challenge had been irresistible when he had thrown the assignment at her and sweetened it with a wager that he knew she couldn't refuse.

When she'd returned from the Mideast six weeks earlier and had to be hospitalized with a bout of malaria, Mac had adamantly refused to give her any further overseas assignments for at least six months. Despite her pleas, threats, and constant nagging, he had remained unmoved for three weeks. Then he'd dangled the lifting of the ban as his part of the wager she was now engaged in. If she lost the bet, she was to accept his edict and cease her efforts to change his mind.

"You were right, Miss McKenna," the security guard said genially, as he stepped from the elevator. "Mr. O'Brien said you were to go right up."

I just bet he did, Kelly thought. "*Step into my parlor,*" *said the spider to the fly*. She squared her shoulders and rewarded the guard with a warm smile. "Thank you, you've been very kind," she said sincerely, stepping into the elevator and pressing the button.

When she got out of the elevator, she took one final deep breath and composed her features into an expression, she hoped, of bland sophistication. Then she knocked firmly on the paneled teak door of O'Brien's apartment. It was opened immediately by the man himself, and Kelly felt her mouth fall open in surprise before she quickly regained her composure.

Nick O'Brien's dazzling good looks were quite familiar to her, for she had been observing him for three weeks, but she had never seen him at such close range or seen quite so *much* of him. The man was wearing nothing but a white bath towel, which was wrapped casually about his hips, and he was as unconcerned as if he were dressed in black tie and tails. Though if more men possessed such overpoweringly virile physiques, perhaps nudity would have been the mode, Kelly thought dazedly. She had never before seen such a gorgeous man. A little over six feet, he was all bronze muscular power. A triangular pelt of springy dark hair covered his broad chest before narrowing to a thin line and disappearing into the towel draped around his hips.

"Enjoying yourself?" O'Brien drawled, and Kelly felt the color flood her face as her gaze flew guiltily from his taut, hard stomach to his face.

"I-I'm sorry," she stammered, moistening her lips nervously. "Did I get you out of the shower? I can wait until you dress." So much for her cool, sophisticated facade, she thought disgustedly. Damn it, why did the man have to be so attractive? His golden bronze complexion and shining, coal black hair reminded her of a modern-day Montezuma. His brilliant aquamarine eyes were startlingly beautiful. From her dossier on him, she knew his mother had been of Mexican descent and his father Irish-American, but who would have believed that the combination would produce this magnetic attractiveness?

His gaze was very sharp as it slowly traveled from the top of her curly blond head to her small booted feet. "I wasn't in the shower," he said coolly. "I'm doing some yoga exercises." Then his gaze fastened on her face, and Kelly felt suddenly that she'd been analyzed, categorized, and was now being filed away somewhere in the computer banks behind that lazy smile. "I admit that I was curious to see what kind of seductress had tempted our stalwart security guard from his post. I was going to look you over, and then I was going to chew you up in little pieces, Miss McKenna."

The last sentence was said with such geniality that Kelly at first thought he was joking until she saw the hard, ruthless curve of his mouth. She bristled indignantly and was about to reply when he threw open the door and stepped aside. "Instead, I think that I'll listen to what you have to say. You're not at all what I expected, Goldilocks. It may prove to be amusing."

Kelly sailed past him regally. Any remorse she might have felt about the distasteful method she'd been forced to use to get to see O'Brien had vanished with his rude arrogance. Goldilocks, indeed!

"How condescending of you, Mr. O'Brien," she said icily, as she walked briskly down the foyer steps into the sunken living room. "I'll try to be entertaining." She was infuriated to hear an amused chuckle behind her, which she pointedly ignored, and proceeded to gaze disdainfully around her. However, as she moved to the center of the room, she found it increasingly difficult to maintain the pose. She was attracted in spite of herself, to the splendidly tranquil beauty of the room.

The decor had a distinctly oriental flavor—ambiguously opulent yet restrained. The plush, ice blue wall-to-wall carpet was the only Western note in a room that was as unusual as the man who had created it. There was no furniture in the room at all except for a lovely low teak table in front of the fireplace. There was a midnight blue velvet mat on the carpet in front of the table; the mat was surrounded by nile green, cerulean, and cream pillows. A bronze screen with beautifully engraved peacocks occupied one corner of the room, and the walls were covered with original paintings obviously chosen for their serenity and delicacy of color.

She turned away from an unusually fine Renoir to say sincerely, "What a heavenly place to live. Is the rest of the apartment like this?"

There was an odd flicker behind his blue eyes. "No, the rest of the apartment is more Western in decor," he said slowly, his eyes on her glowing face. "I find a blend of cultures suits me better than a total devotion to one." He gestured mockingly to the midnight blue velvet mat. "Won't you sit down? You'll find it surprisingly comfortable."

Kelly seated herself carefully, her eyes fixed warily on O'Brien as he dropped gracefully down beside her. It seemed that her offer to wait until O'Brien was more suitably dressed was being ignored; his nudity obviously didn't bother him at all. She wished that she could say the same. The proximity of all that virile muscular flesh was having a most peculiar effect on her heartbeat and respiration. She drew a deep breath hoping that O'Brien had not noticed. It seemed that he hadn't, for his gaze was fixed with definite admiration on the expanse of silken thighs revealed by the slit in her skirt. Kelly instinctively tried to draw the skirt closed, but it was impossible in her half-reclining position.

"You know, I may decide to redecorate the rest of the apartment, after all," he said, his eyes still on her naked thighs. "It's beginning to look increasingly attractive to me."

Kelly gave up the battle with the skirt and looked up at him crossly. "It may be lovely, but it's definitely not meant for western apparel. Don't your guests find it a bit awkward?"

He shrugged, then leaned back against the pillows. "On the contrary, I find it relaxes them and is much more conducive to the lowering of social barriers." His lips quirked slightly. "It's a little like going back to the womb. Haven't you noticed how children gravitate naturally to the earth? It's practically instinctive for them to avoid chairs in favor of the floor."

"I hadn't realized that," Kelly said thoughtfully. "But you're right. I remember that as a child my father was always telling me to get off the floor and sit properly like a lady."

"And that was such a long time ago," O'Brien scoffed gently, his gaze on the glossy, sun-streaked curls that framed her face. "You're not much more than a baby now."

Kelly bristled indignantly and tried to draw herself up haughtily. Unfortunately, she found the move only further opened the slit in her skirt, a fact that added to her displeasure. "That was some time ago, actually," she said coolly. "I'm twenty-three years old, Mr. O'Brien, and I've been a photojournalist since I was nineteen. If you'd care to check my credentials, you'll find that I'm quite respected in my profession."

"Oh, I thoroughly approve of your credentials," he said mischievously, his gaze returning to her thighs. "Although I'm not at all sure of your ethics." He picked up the envelope that he had dropped on the low teak table and waved it at her carelessly. "I believe that blackmail tactics are still frowned upon by most responsible journalists."

Kelly flushed and bit her lip, her jade green eyes wide with distress. "How would you know?" she asked belligerently. "You haven't seen fit to give any of us an interview since you were sixteen, Mr. O'Brien. That hardly makes you a competent judge."

O'Brien's lips thinned, and his expression became bitter. "You think not? I was a qualified expert on the members of your profession while you were still in diapers, Goldilocks. I had to put up with the circus they made of my life when I was a child, but I'll never be put in that position again."

"You couldn't expect the media to just ignore you," Kelly responded. "You were news. How many geniuses of your caliber do you think appear in a generation? For that matter, how many appear in a century? Your IQ ran right off the scale, and by the time you were ten, educators were comparing you to Einstein. You graduated from college when you were twelve and received your doctorate in computer engineering when you were fifteen. For heaven's sake, you were a phenomenon!"

"I was a freak," he said tersely, his aquamarine eyes brooding. "And thanks to the media, I was a very well publicized one—as you have just proven by rattling off the facts of my life. It didn't occur to the media that I was also a child and didn't know a damn thing about how to handle a problem on that scale. I was just lucky I learned before I went around the bend."

Kelly felt a twinge of guilt at the thought of that confused little boy. Then she dismissed the thought. There was nothing in the least pitiful in this outrageously attractive male next to her.

"You seem to have thrived despite our insensitive handling of your delicate feelings, Mr. O'Brien. You scarcely can say that you've led a retiring life despite your aversion to publicity. You're only in your late twenties, yet you're practically a legend in your own time. The larger than life, fabulous Nick O'Brien."

O'Brien's eyes narrowed to icy blue slits. "You seem to have done your homework at least, Miss McKenna. I'd be curious to know what else you've discovered about my murky past." He gestured to the envelope. "Besides this little item, of course."

Kelly moistened her lips nervously before saying decisively, "I'd hardly be a competent reporter if I'd neglected to research you thoroughly before approaching you, Mr. O'Brien, though most of it was pretty well cut and dried. If I may continue 'rattling off the facts' of your life, you're the only son of Michael O'Brien, head of O'Brien Computer Corporation. Your mother died when you were two, and you were raised by your father and a number of qualified tutors. You have a photographic memory, which must have been a great help in your education because you have a string of letters after your name. You've made several advances in computer technology in the past ten years, and you've recently developed some little chip or something that everyone says will completely revolutionize the industry." She looked at him gravely. "There's even talk about a possible Nobel Prize nomination."

"As you say, pretty well cut and dried," he said coolly. "But I'd venture to guess that you've delved deeper than my academic background."

She nodded, her eyes shifting away from him to rest on the misty Renoir on the wall. "Your private life is just as newsworthy, Mr. O'Brien. You've been something of a daredevil since you were in your teens. Skydiving. Rodeo bronc busting. Race cars. You like to take chances, and so far you've been lucky. There was, of course, the time you were shot when you arranged to rescue those American oil men who were being held hostage after the revolution in Said Ababa. But that was only in the shoulder and hardly counts, does it?"

"You overestimate my Spartan endurance. It ached damnably for about two months and was stiff for another three." His eyes were fixed with amused speculation on her face. "You must have very good sources. If I remember correctly, that particular episode was never publicized. The State Department was a bit touchy about the rescue since they were negotiating sub rosa for a treaty with the new regime."

Kelly's eyes twinkled impishly. "A certain amount of guesswork on my part," she admitted. "But I'm glad to hear it confirmed."

O'Brien chuckled, a glint of admiration flickering briefly in his eyes. "Strictly off the record, Goldilocks. Officially that airlift never happened. I don't suppose you'd like to tell me how you managed to uncover my tracks?"

She shook her head firmly, and he chuckled again. "I didn't think so." Then his smile slowly faded as he removed the black and white photograph from the envelope and tossed it on her lap. "Now, suppose we get down to brass tacks," he said grimly. "I believe this photograph was meant to open negotiations?"

Kelly was jerked back to reality with a vengeance by the abrupt change in O'Brien's manner. From lazy, almost indulgent good humor, he had switched with lightning swiftness to the dangerous alertness of a stalking panther. She had almost been lured into actually enjoying his easy camaraderie. Which only went to prove that the man was even more dangerous than she'd imagined.

She picked up the picture and glanced at it. "It's really a good shot, isn't it?" she asked coolly. "I was quite proud of it. If ever a picture tells a story, this one does." She had taken the photo of O'Brien and his voluptuous female companion at a small French restaurant a few nights before.

"A hand on a lady's thigh hardly constitutes a compromising situation," he said. "Perhaps I was merely being platonically affectionate."

"The look Señora Dominguez is giving you was almost hot enough to melt the film in my camera," Kelly said bluntly. "You left the restaurant five minutes later, without waiting for your dinner, and returned to this apartment. Señora Dominguez didn't leave until ten the next morning."

"And you were waiting outside all that time?" O'Brien asked. "You should have come on up, Goldilocks. I can't say that I'm overly fond of *ménage à trois*, but I just might have made an exception in your case."

Kelly could feel the hot color stain her cheeks. "I'm not concerned with your love affairs, Mr. O'Brien. I'm sure you've had more mistresses than even my expert research can substantiate. The only reason I took the photograph is that I needed a lever, and I thought this might prove the only one I could use."

"Oh, what a wicked blow to my self-esteem." O'Brien mockingly arched his brow. "And I thought you were shivering outside all night long in a fever of lust for my virile young body."

Damn the man, Kelly thought vexedly, and damn this blasted habit she had of lighting up like a Christmas tree at the slightest provocation. How could she maintain the image of a hard-bitten cynical newspaperwoman when she still blushed like a schoolgirl?

"Hardly," she retorted. "You seemed to be very well taken care of by Señora Dominguez."

"Yes, I believe I was at that," O'Brien agreed, a reminiscent grin on his face. "But you needn't be jealous, sweetheart. I've always preferred blonds."

"Actually, your track record displays a leaning toward brunettes by almost two to one," Kelly corrected.

"Well, there are blonds," he said, his blue eyes twinkling mischievously as he reached out and tugged at a curl, "and then there are *blonds*."

She pulled away from his hand. "You needn't waste your sexual expertise on me, Mr. O'Brien. Judging from your reputation, I'm sure that it's spread fairly thin already. You'd do better to ask me what I intend to do with that photograph."

"All right, Goldilocks," he said obligingly. "What do you intend to do with that photograph?"

She gritted her teeth in frustration. This interview was not going at all as she'd imagined. O'Brien did not appear to be the least bit worried about his liaison with Maria Dominguez. In fact, he seemed to be outrageously amused by the entire affair. Or perhaps that was a front, she thought speculatively. Well, she would just have to pursue it further and see if he showed any signs of annoyance or anxiety.

She drew a deep breath and said in a little rush,

"Señora Dominguez is the wife of the minister of finance of an important oil-rich country in South America. I doubt very much if the State Department would be pleased if your little affair threatened the negotiations for their oil reserves." She moistened her lips nervously. "Based on your new discovery, the Pentagon has just signed a gigantic contract for O'Brien computers. It's possible that they might even cancel the agreement if the State Department applied enough pressure."

O'Brien's eyes were narrowed and no longer lazy. "I see," he said slowly. "And you're threatening to reveal my little indiscretion if I don't give in to what you want?"

Kelly nodded, hoping those piercing blue eyes would not see through her bluff. "That's right," she said lightly. "However, if you agree to my demands, I'll give you all the negatives and also my solemn promise to forget I ever saw Señora Dominguez with you."

"Very generous," O'Brien said dryly. "And just what do you want from me?"

Here goes, Kelly thought, taking a deep breath. "Next week you're testing a new fuel that a chemist friend of yours invented. You're planning on riding a hot air balloon from the Rio Grande valley to Acapulco. I want to go with you."

"That's all?" O'Brien asked, his blue eyes wary.

"That's enough. It would be quite a scoop for any reporter, Mr. O'Brien, particularly since you're so media shy."

"You've gone to a great deal of trouble to catch me in your little trap," he said thoughtfully, his eyes on her tense, eager face. "I wonder why it's so important to you."

"I just told you," Kelly said, evading his piercing glance. "I want to get a story."

"Perhaps," he said absently, his eyes on the color that was again mounting to her cheeks. "But I don't think that was the entire reason, was it? Now, let me see. What do I remember about one Kelly Mc-Kenna? You have a very memorable face, sweetheart. It should be easy to retrieve the facts to go with that face."

Oh, Lord, the man had a photographic memory, Kelly thought uneasily. There was little chance that he would fail to make the connection. "Don't waste your time, Mr. O'Brien," she said with forced lightness. "I'm always behind the camera, not in front of it."

"Not always, Goldilocks," he corrected. "You were very much in front of the camera in Frankfurt three years ago. In fact, you made the cover of every weekly news magazine in the country. You were quite the little heroine."

"Bull. I was an unknown reporter who saw a way to get an exclusive that would get me national attention. Self-serving, perhaps, but hardly heroic."

"But the public didn't see it that way, did they? They only saw a dainty, golden-haired Joan of Arc who marched bravely up the steps of the American embassy where twelve hostages were being held captive by terrorists. They heard her offer to exchange places with one of the hostages and saw a very frightened young secretary go free. You were only twenty years old and had everything to live for. There wasn't a dry eye in any living room in America when you disappeared into that embassy." His lips twisted mockingly. "It was all very touching."

"You evidently didn't share their concern," Kelly said. "Weren't *you* moved by my plight?"

"Oh, yes, I was moved," he said quietly. "I was probably more terrified for you than any of those kindly souls who built a halo over your little head because I felt a certain empathy with you. It was as if I were in that embassy with you sharing your terror and your excitement."

"Excitement?"

"You don't have to pretend with me, sweetheart,"

he said. "There was a brief close-up of you on that live TV news broadcast as you were talking to the terrorist leader right before you marched into that embassy. I might have been looking into a mirror. I'm not the only one who likes to take chances, am I, Kelly McKenna?"

"I don't know what you're talking about," Kelly said, hoping she sounded convincing. "I told you that it was strictly ambition raising its ugly head. I saw a chance to make a smart career move, and I took it." There was no way that she was going to admit to this dangerous man how well he had read her, even though she felt strangely pleased that he not only understood but had actually shared her emotions.

"You're something of a freak yourself, Kelly, love. You're an addict on the oldest drug in existence. You love to feel the adrenaline flow when you're scared half out of your mind, don't you? You love walking on the tightrope with the lions waiting and hungry below you."

"That's crazy. I take chances because it's my job, not because I enjoy it."

O'Brien shook his dark head. "We both know what we are, Kelly. But you shouldn't have involved yourself in a no-win situation like the one in Frankfurt. That came pretty close to suicide."

"Nonsense. All the hostages were released at the airport, just as the terrorists promised."

"You were lucky, and you know it," O'Brien said bluntly. "It could have just as well gone the other way." He gave her a long, thoughtful look, which caused Kelly to shift uneasily. "I believe that I'm going to have to take you under my wing, Kelly. It's too dangerous to have you running around loose."

"I've been taking care of myself for over five years and done a fairly competent job of it, Mr. O'Brien," Kelly said curtly. "I don't feel I need your help at this late date."

"Five years," O'Brien repeated softly. "That's right. Your father died when you were eighteen, didn't he? He was Richard McKenna, a free-lance photographer who traveled all over the world taking action shots that are still regarded by some as the best ever photographed. You must have been very proud of him."

"Yes, very proud," Kelly said simply. "He was a great photographer and a wonderful father. After my mother died when I was eight, he saw that we were never separated until the day he died. He took me with him wherever he went."

"It's no wonder you're an addict, sweetheart. You've had years to develop that habit." He held up his hand to halt her indignant reply. "Okay, I'll drop the discussion of your little problem if you'll tell me why it was so important for you to get this assignment."

"I told you that—" Kelly started.

"I'd appreciate it if you'd cut out the bull and level with me," O'Brien interrupted. "The Kelly Mc-Kenna I read about three years ago wouldn't deal in blackmail."

Kelly bit her lip uncertainly before she decided to be frank with him. It probably couldn't do any harm to her case. The man practically knew her whole life history anyway. "I had a bet with my editor that I'd get you to take me along," she confessed hesitantly.

"Interesting," O'Brien said, his eyes narrowing on her face. "And the stakes?"

She was not about to confess that it was the return of her overseas assignments. He was already convinced that she was some kind of danger junkie. "Something that I wanted very much," Kelly said evasively, not looking at him.

"And if you lose?" he asked quietly, his eyes on the guilty color that was staining her cheeks.

"Then I give him something that he wants very much," she said, still not looking at him. If she had, she would have noticed the sudden tenseness of his shoulders and the flicker that might have been anger in his blue eyes.

"I see," he said flatly. "The oldest bargain in history and certainly the most intriguing." Kelly looked up in confusion, but he didn't notice her expression. "Well, I believe that I'll see that your boss doesn't take home the marbles this time, Goldilocks. I'm taking you with me."

"You will!" Kelly said excitedly, her face glowing. "That's wonderful! You won't regret it. I promise that I won't be any trouble, and I'll let you approve any material that I write about you."

"You're damn right you will. And any pictures that you take as well." He stood up lithely and reached down to pull her to her feet.

Now that the decision was made, it seemed that the man couldn't wait to send her on her way, Kelly thought. "Of course," she said. "That goes without saying. Thank you again, Mr. O'Brien."

"Nick," he said curtly. "Formality is a bit absurd within the confines of a hot air balloon, don't you think?"

"Nick," she repeated softly, the name tripping with strange intimacy off her tongue. "Yes, I suppose it is. You'll be in touch with me sometime next week then?"

"I like the way you say my name in that husky little voice," he said, his eyes oddly intent on her face. "I'd like to hear you murmur—" He broke off abruptly and shook his head as if to clear it. "Next week?"

"You'll be leaving for the Rio Grande valley for the ascent next week," Kelly reminded him. "Isn't that the plan?"

He was still staring at her face, his gaze lingering on the curve of her lower lip. Kelly was almost mesmerized by the intensity of that stare, and she felt an odd heat surge through her.

"No," he said abruptly, turning away and moving

briskly toward the foyer. "We're leaving tonight. I'll be by to pick you up at nine. Be ready. What's your address?"

"Tonight!" Kelly protested, following closely on his heels. "But that's impossible. I can't be ready to go tonight. Why the change in plans?"

"Because I feel like it," O'Brien said. "Didn't your research cover the fact that all geniuses are eccentric? If you want to go with me, be ready to go at nine."

"But I have a dinner engagement," Kelly said crossly. "I just can't break a date without any warning. Can't you wait at least until tomorrow?"

"No, I can't," he said crisply, as he turned at the front door to look down at her. "What date is so important that you can't put it off for this dynamite story that you're so eager to get? Is it with your editor?"

"Mac?" Kelly said bewilderedly. "No, it's Simon Renwick. He's in the advertising department at *World Weekly*."

O'Brien's lips curved unpleasantly. "You *are* a busy little girl, aren't you?" he said. "Well, he'll have to do without your services tonight, Goldilocks. You can either get rid of him before I pick you up, or I'll take care of it when I get there. I really wouldn't advise you to leave it up to me, though. I'm feeling a bit savage today."

That was more than obvious, Kelly thought. It seemed that geniuses were not only eccentric but downright moody. She couldn't imagine what had put O'Brien in such a temper, but he looked as fierce as one of his Aztec ancestors, and she didn't want to stick around and be a pagan sacrifice to that wrath.

"Okay," she agreed, then sighed. "I'll be ready at nine." She gave him her street address and apartment number.

"Good," he said tersely, opening the door for her. "I'd advise you to wear something a bit more practical than that outfit you have on. It may be May, but it can get quite cool in a balloon."

"I do have a little common sense. May I suggest that you follow your own advice? I'd say you're far less practically dressed than I!" She gazed pointedly at the white towel draped carelessly about his hips. "Or perhaps all that yoga has trained you to control your body temperature."

He grinned, his blue eyes dancing and his bad temper suddenly banished by amusement. "Actually, that was one of the first things I learned when I studied with the Buddhist monks in Tibet two years ago," he replied blandly. "Didn't my dossier delve into those six months, sweetheart? Right now I'm working on controlling the flow of blood to the organs without the benefit of the heart pumping it."

"You mean you're trying to stop your heart from beating?" she asked, her eyes widening in surprise.

"Only temporarily. It will probably take years for me to reach anywhere near the competence of the monks. A master can totally cease his heartbeat for more than thirty minutes."

"That's wonderful," Kelly said faintly. "I don't quite see why you would want to stop your heart from beating, but I'm sure you'll succeed if you persevere."

O'Brien smiled, his white teeth flashing brilliantly in his dark face. "It's the challenge, love. It's a key to be found and a puzzle to be solved." He pushed her out the door with a gentle swat on her derriere. "Nine o'clock," he reminded her, then shut the door firmly in her face.

Two

Oh, Lord, why did things like this always happen to her? Kelly wondered gloomily, as she watched Simon Renwick and Paúl Lautner square off. She had always known that Simon was a bit on the macho side, but who would have believed that slight, bespectacled Paul would display this ferocity?

"Look, it's all very simple," Kelly said soothingly, as she stepped between the two men. "I just got a little confused on my appointments and made two dates for the same night. I'm sorry that it happened, but there's not much I can do about it, and—"

"No one's blaming you for the mix-up, doll," Simon growled, his eyes on Paul's angry face. "You just leave it to us to sort it out. Why don't you get your jacket and meet me downstairs in the foyer?"

Doll. If there was one endearment she hated, it was that one, Kelly thought. Why had she accepted the date with Simon, anyway? His athletic, blond good looks now appeared a bit too obvious and wholesome and his charm much too facile and slick.

"That's a good idea, Kelly," Paul said, his thin, intelligent face flushed with rage. "I'll join you in a minute." The entire mix-up was really more his fault than Simon's, Kelly thought disgustedly. If he hadn't looked so hungry and generally uncared for, she would never have invited him to her apartment for a home-cooked meal when he'd dropped into the office the previous week between assignments. Paul was a well-known journalist, but he usually looked as rumpled as an unmade bed, and he had the soulful eyes of a hungry spaniel.

Kelly shook her head. There was really no use trying to shift the blame when she knew this awkwardness was the result of her own blasted absentmindedness. Simon hadn't been in his office in the afternoon, and she had been so busy making arrangements that she had forgotten to call him at home to cancel the date. And she had completely forgotten about the date with Paul. They had arrived simultaneously at her front door five minutes ago. Not only had she not been able to get a word in edgewise to explain that she couldn't go out with either one of them that night, but they had become so antagonistic that she was afraid they might come to blows at any moment.

"Look, there's something that I've got to explain to both of you," Kelly said desperately. "I—"

"You'd best stay out of this, doll," Simon said, placing his hands on her slender waist and shifting her to one side. "Don't you worry your pretty little head about a thing."

She could have slapped his smug, good-looking face. Pretty little head, indeed!

"If you'd listen to what I have to say," she said angrily, "you'd see just how ridiculous you're both acting."

They both stared at her in surprise mixed with

resentment. She could almost feel the shift of antagonism from each other toward her. Well, why not? She certainly deserved it, and it was far better that they be angry with her than attempt to mutilate each other.

"You both have a perfect right to be irritated with me," she said earnestly. "And I hope you'll believe—" Her abject apology was interrupted by the strident buzz of the doorbell, and she sighed in profound exasperation. She didn't even have to glance at the clock to guess who was at the door. All she needed was another domineering man on the scene!

And Nick O'Brien looked a thousand times more dangerous than the other two men put together, she thought as she opened the door. He was dressed in black; tight black jeans, long-sleeved black sport shirt, and black suede desert boots. He had all the sleek, dangerous litheness of a panther. Well, she was in the mood to let the intimidating Mr. O'Brien do his stuff.

"Hello, Nick," she said breezily, stepping aside to let him enter. "I'm not quite ready." She strolled jauntily past Paul and Simon, who had turned distinctly menacing looks on the new arrival. "Entertain yourselves, won't you?"

She closed the bedroom door behind her and leaned on it for an instant, her head cocked to listen for any outbreak of actual violence. She breathed a sigh of relief when she heard only the low murmur of voices. She felt a twinge of guilt as she hurried into the bathroom to tidy her hair and grab her toothbrush and face cream from the vanity shelf. It was not exactly fair of her to leave O'Brien in this tricky spot, but she'd had more than enough of coping with unreasonable males for one evening. Besides, he *had* offered to rid her of Renwick's presence if he was still there when he arrived. As a matter of fact, it had been more of a threat than an offer, she thought, grinning impishly. He had said that he liked challenges. She'd merely provided him with a little more than he'd bargained for.

She was striding back to the bedroom when she halted abruptly. Her ring! She turned and hurried back into the bathroom and retrieved the dainty jade and gold ring from the plastic vanity tray on which she had placed it before taking her shower. Sighing in relief, she slid it on her finger. It would have been a minor disaster if she'd forgotten her lucky ring on this particular jaunt. She had an idea that a woman would need all the luck she could get on a hot air balloon trip with a man like Nick O'Brien.

It took only five minutes to finish packing her zippered khaki duffel bag. She carefully put her Leica camera into the bag along with several rolls of film. She had changed into olive green denim jeans and matching long-sleeved shirt before Paul and Simon had arrived, and it took only another moment to change into her dark green canvas shoes and grab up her white leather jacket.

At the bedroom door she stopped for a moment and listened anxiously for any sounds of turbulence from the living room. It was almost ominously quiet, and her brow creased in a perplexed frown. She flipped off the bedroom light, then peered out cautiously into the living room. It was deserted.

"I just checked to make sure all your appliances were turned off," O'Brien said briskly, as he strolled out of the kitchen. "Do you have any regular deliveries? Milk? Newspapers?"

Kelly shook her head. "No. And my next-door neighbor will collect my mail while I'm gone." She looked warily around the apartment. Where the devil were Paul and Simon?

"Good," O'Brien said tersely, taking her duffel bag and propelling her toward the front door. "Let's get out of here." He flipped off the living room light, closed the door, and waited while she locked it. "We'll take the company jet as far as Brownsville," he said casually, as he crossed the hall and pressed the button for the elevator. "I have the pilot standing by at the airport."

"How did you get rid of them?" Kelly burst out, unable to contain herself any longer, her jade eyes wide with curiosity.

"Your two belligerent lovers? Well, I didn't throw them out the window, if that's what you're worried about." His vivid blue eyes were distinctly cool as they regarded her. "That's really all you're entitled to know, Goldilocks. You opted out of the situation, remember?"

Kelly looked away guiltily. "Well, you did offer your services," she reminded him. The doors of the elevator slid open, and they quickly entered, but she was not prepared for the overwhelming intimacy she felt when the doors slid shut enclosing her in the narrow space with him. Nick stood looking down at her, his face oddly hard and stern. He was so close that she could see the pulse beat in the hollow of his throat and smell the warm, clean scent of soap and a vaguely woodsy fragrance that she thought must be his shaving lotion.

"And you took advantage of them," he said slowly. His hand reached out to stroke the silky curve of her cheek, and she inhaled sharply at the almost electric shock she'd received from that casual touch. "But I never said that the offer was without strings. You owe me, Kelly, and I always collect."

"Not very gallant," she said, laughing shakily and moistening her lips nervously. "I would have taken care of the matter myself if I'd known you'd get so uptight about it."

"I don't like being used, and I detest being set up," he said curtly, and at her shocked protest, his eyes zeroed in on her with the cutting force of a laser ray. "Don't even try to deny it, Kelly. You received a little too much pleasure out of turning me loose on your ardent admirers. You wanted to see how I'd react to the sight of you surrounded by your lovers. Did it excite you to know that you'd aroused the caveman in all of us, Kelly?"

"You're crazy. I only wanted you to get them to leave so that I could get on with my job." She could feel the tears brimming in her eyes. Why did it hurt so much to realize that he thought of her as some kind of unfeeling vamp? The man meant absolutely nothing to her.

O'Brien studied her tear-bright eyes and pale, taut face for a long moment before his hand resumed its leisurely stroking motion. "Poor baby," he said gently. "I don't think you even realized it yourself. Can't you see that you wanted to provoke a response from me even if it was a violent one? I can't let you keep doing that, Kelly. I've never had the coolest temperament anyway, and you seem to be able to stir me up without trying. Prod me too far, and I won't care if I hurt you or not."

Kelly shook her head, her jade eyes clouded with bewilderment. "You're wrong, Nick. I wouldn't do anything like that." She couldn't be that sort of sensation seeker, could she? She had a fleeting memory of that surge of impish triumph she'd felt when she had left Nick in that room with those two angry men, and she felt suddenly sick.

"You won't be doing it anymore," O'Brien said quietly. "Because we're going to be closer than Siamese twins, Goldilocks, and I know you better than you do yourself. There aren't going to be any more no-win situations for you, Kelly." The elevator doors slid silently open, and Nick took her arm and propelled her firmly through the lobby toward the glass entrance doors. "And if you bring me face to face with any other of your ex-lovers, I'll probably murder them," he said grimly.

• • •

"Is there anything I can do to help?" Kelly shouted over the roar of the burners.

O'Brien looked up from his intent scanning of the altimeter to give her a smile. "Just relax and enjoy," he shouted back. "I have to keep an eye on these burners for a bit. If we climb too rapidly, the air resistance could cause the balloon to split."

"What a pleasant thought," Kelly replied sarcastically, moving to the side of the wicker gondola to peer down at the Rio Grande valley far below. It looked just like a painting by Grandma Moses from this height, she mused, all patchwork green and brown. Her gaze moved up anxiously to the brilliant scarlet balloon blossoming above her like an enormous mushroom. Propelled by the hot air generated by the burners, the balloon was soaring like a toy released by a child's careless hand.

But there had been nothing careless about their ascension. It had taken six men to restrain and hold the billowing chute open after the burners had been lit until it was time to heave the gondola into the air.

The air was growing rapidly cooler, and Kelly slipped on her jacket and zippered it before reaching into her duffel bag for her camera. For the next five minutes she occupied herself with shooting the interior of their six-foot-square gondola and then, with considerably more interest, O'Brien's dark, intent face and taut, alert form. Against the stunning blue backdrop of the sky, he appeared even more aggressively masculine.

O'Brien looked up briefly, and raised an eyebrow, but her snapping shutter received no further attention. It was only when he noticed her seated on the rim of the gondola with only one arm around the metal strut for balance that he protested. And it was a silent protest; he gave her a ferocious, menacing frown and gestured abruptly with one hand.

After grimacing at him, Kelly reluctantly climbed

down and leaned against the side of the basket, where she continued to shoot pictures. She was startled out of her absorption with her task by the sudden absence of any sound. O'Brien had turned off the burners.

"We've reached fifteen thousand feet," he explained, as he reached for his black flight jacket and pulled it on. "We'll only need to use the burners occasionally from now on. Our optimum altitude is seventeen thousand, and the wind will carry us the remaining two thousand feet."

"Wind?" Kelly asked doubtfully. The balloon was still in motion, but she felt a curiously weightless, drifting sensation. "Are you sure there is one?"

O'Brien smiled. "Quite a strong one, as a matter of fact," he assured her. "You don't notice it because the winds are so silent at this altitude."

"Is that it?" Kelly asked, looking out the gondola at the terrain far below. "I suppose you're right. It's unbelievably quiet up here. I've never known such a completely peaceful atmosphere." She looked up at the brilliant scarlet chute above them. "It's enormous, isn't it?" she asked eagerly, "Are all hot air balloons this size?"

"No, this one isn't all that big. It's slightly smaller than average," O'Brien replied, leaning against one of the metal struts and watching her glowing face with evident enjoyment. "It's about sixty-six thousand cubic feet. They run as large as eighty-seven thousand cubic feet. If I'd known I was going to have a passenger, I'd have arranged for more roomy accommodations."

"To tell you the truth, I'm finding our little nest quite cozy," Kelly said flippantly over her shoulder. "Do you usually fly this thing solo?"

"Well, I meant to tell you about that," he said, his blue eyes dancing with mischief. "Actually, I've only been up in a hot air balloon once before and then only for about a three-hour trip."

"I beg your pardon," Kelly said blankly, turning

slowly to face him. She couldn't have heard him correctly. Even Nick O'Brien wouldn't have attempted anything so outrageous. "Would you mind repeating that?"

O'Brien nodded. "This is the first time I've taken a balloon up solo," he repeated cheerfully. "I felt I should have some sort of instruction, so I hired an experienced balloonist to show me the ropes the first time, of course."

"Of course," Kelly echoed faintly, gazing into his face, which was alight with mischief. "You're putting me on, aren't you?"

He shook his dark head decisively. "Nope," he said. "I would have told you before, but you seemed so eager to come along that I hated to dampen your enthusiasm. How are you enjoying your first balloon ride, Goldilocks?"

"Very much, thank you," she said dazedly. Then, incredibly, she began to chuckle, and her chuckle quickly escalated into uproarious laughter. Holding her sides, she sank to the floor of the gondola and leaned against the wicker wall.

"You're not hysterical, are you?" O'Brien asked warily, his gaze narrowing on her brimming eyes and flushed face. "I've got to warn you that a six-foot gondola is no place for a hysterical woman. I just might have to toss you overboard."

"You'd probably do it, too." She was having difficulty speaking coherently through the helpless giggles that were still shaking her. "And *you* accused me of involving myself in no-win situations! I'm now floating some seventeen thousand feet above the ground with a totally inexperienced pilot who is using an equally untested fuel to propel us to sunny Acapulco in a gaudy scarlet hot air balloon." She shook her head, still chuckling. "Can you blame me for losing my cool?"

"My balloon is not gaudy," he defended. "And you didn't lose your cool, sweetheart. You laughed." He shook his head wonderingly. "Any other woman would have been screaming hysterically or in an old-fashioned Victorian swoon right now. Do you know how long I've looked for a woman like you?"

Kelly's green eyes were dancing as they met his across the expanse of the basket. "I hope you don't set up tests like these too frequently, Nick," she said dryly. "The next woman you decide to take ballooning may not be as amused."

He smiled slowly with a warm intimacy that caused Kelly's breath to catch oddly in her chest. "But why should I take another woman with me, love?" he asked gently. "I'll never find another Kelly McKenna to laugh with me."

Kelly found she couldn't answer; she was suddenly breathlessly shy. It seemed that the total silence around them was enfolding the two of them in their own intimate world and Kelly could almost hear the throbbing of her heart. She tore her eyes from O'Brien's face and fixed her gaze desperately on the burners beside him. "Would it be too much to ask if you know how to get this thing back down on the ground?" she asked.

O'Brien smiled. He was looking at her with a glowing tenderness that made her feel bewildered. "Of course," he said simply. "I'd never have taken you along if I hadn't been entirely confident that I could take care of you." His lips curved in a wry smile. "I can't give you similar assurance about the fuel formula, but the premise the inventor used is sound."

"That's comforting to know," Kelly said, making a face. "Why did it have to be tested in a hot air balloon?"

His answering grin was impish. "Why not?" He shrugged. "I thought it might be amusing."

Kelly chuckled again, shaking her head in resignation. What other answer had she expected from an outrageous eccentric like Nick O'Brien? If she had any sense at all, she'd be half out of her mind with terror. Instead, she felt an odd serenity at O'Brien's firm assurance that her safety was in his hands. Strange. She had not felt so secure and protected even when her father had been alive.

"Why not?" she echoed, returning his smile. "What do we do while we see if your friend's fuel is going to keep us airborne?"

She could have bitten her tongue as O'Brien lifted his eyebrows. His smile became wickedly mischievous. "I'm tempted to give you the obvious answer, but I'll try to restrain myself. I think you've had enough of a shock for one morning." He sank down on the floor across from her, crossing his legs Indian fashion. "Ballooning is a lazy man's sport, Kelly. I hope you brought a good book?"

She felt exceedingly lucky to get off nearly unscathed after the opening she had given him, and she hurriedly rummaged through her bag and pulled out a paperback thriller. "I have!" she said triumphantly, holding up the book. "What are you going to do?"

He pulled some papers out of his own brown cowhide satchel, and leaned against the side of the gondola lazily, propping a yellow pad of paper on his knees. "I'm a puzzle addict," he said, his brow already knitted in concentration as he gazed down at the papers in front of him. "I thought I'd try to get a couple of these deciphered while I had the time."

Kelly sighed resignedly. "I take it you don't mean *The New York Times* crossword puzzle?"

"What?" he looked up, his pale blue eyes absorbed. "No," he said. "The Pentagon lets me play with some of their stuff occasionally. I find it a trifle more challenging."

Kelly's eyes widened. "The Pentagon? You mean like the CIA? James Bond type stuff?"

O'Brien shook his head. "Sorry to disappoint you, sweetheart, but it's all pretty uninteresting. Nary a Goldfinger or Pussy Galore in the lot."

"Perhaps there are no Goldfingers, but I wouldn't bet on the absence of a Ms. Galore in your circle of acquaintances," Kelly replied. "Your track record indicates a distinct leaning in that direction. Señora Dominguez would have been right at home with 007." Despite her attempt at lightness, there was a trace of tartness in her tone as she recalled the sultry voluptuousness of the South American woman.

Evidently O'Brien detected the subtle undercurrents beneath the remark, for his eyes gleamed teasingly. "Yes, I suppose she would," he said, tilting his head consideringly. "But she wouldn't have lasted long with him. Maria is much too obvious to retain any long-term fascination."

Kelly tried to hide the satisfaction she felt at his careless remark. "How ungrateful of you. I gather you didn't admire the lady for her brilliant mind."

"Actually, the only portion of her anatomy that I was enamored with were her breasts. The rest was strictly mediocre."

For a moment Kelly didn't know whether she was more shocked at his open discussion of his former mistress or at her own resentment of his partiality for an attribute with which she was not generously endowed.

"Personally, I think she's a trifle overblown," Kelly said loftily, opening her book decisively and gluing her eyes blindly to the first page.

She heard O'Brien's pleased chuckle. "I believe you're right at that. I find myself definitely drawn more to quality than to quantity of late." She did not need to look up to know that his gaze was running lingeringly over her breasts. Despite her conscientious attempt to ignore his provocative words, she could feel the pink steal up to her cheeks. O'Brien's chuckle was triumphant.

She purposely did not again lift her eyes, and soon she heard the rustle of the yellow pad on O'Brien's lap. It was another ten minutes until she felt it safe to stop pretending to read. Peeking from beneath her long lashes, she stared at O'Brien's intent face. She needn't have been so careful, she thought ruefully. O'Brien's attention was so concentrated on his task that he didn't know she was in the same world, much less the same gondola. Her gaze ran lingeringly over the lean, almost barbaric beauty of his strong, well-defined features. Lord, a man had no right to be that gorgeous, she thought.

But it was his expression that sent an odd twinge through her. She wondered if he had ever looked at a woman with that same excitement and intensity of purpose that he was devoting to his papers. Well, why should she care if there was a woman somewhere who could invoke that type of response in Nick O'Brien? She scarcely knew the man, and they certainly had nothing in common. Who could possibly be attracted to a man of O'Brien's incredible mental powers and accomplishments? she wondered crossly. It would be like snuggling up to a master computer. So what if he was the most sexually magnetic man she had ever run across in her twenty-three years? He was a man who constantly had to be challenged, who was always making new discoveries; he was bound to become bored and restless with any woman in a relatively short period of time. No, she must take great care to guard herself against that potent charm that was already eroding her resistance and leaving her bewildered and slightly dazzled.

Despite her stern self-admonition, for the remainder of the morning and early afternoon she found both her gaze and attention returning again and again to that quiet, frowning figure sitting tailor fashion across from her. Except for the occasions when he roused himself to check the altimeter and start the burners for short periods, he was entirely absorbed in whatever he was working on. Instead of following her stern resolve to concentrate on her novel, she found herself listening with almost maternal amusement to O'Brien's absent mutterings and occasional chuckles of triumph. She was not aware at what point she gave up entirely, dropped the paperback, and curled up with her head pillowed on her crossed arms to gaze at O'Brien. Nor was she conscious of the exact time when her eyes fluttered shut and she fell peacefully asleep.

Three

When Kelly opened her eyes again, it was to see O'Brien sitting quietly, his pad and pen put away and his gaze on her. "Hi," he said softly. "I'm glad you're awake. I was getting lonely." He stretched lazily. "How about some dinner? You haven't eaten all day, but I figured that you needed the rest more than sustenance after your broken sleep last night. You only catnapped on the plane from San Francisco."

"I never sleep well on jets," Kelly said, yawning. She sat up and ran her hand through her tousled curls. "Though I seem to have no trouble at all in balloons. It was like being rocked in a cradle. How long have I been asleep?"

"All afternoon." O'Brien reached for a wicker picnic hamper beside the burners. "It's almost sundown, or I would have let you sleep longer. I didn't want you to miss the sunset. It's fairly spectacular up here." He passed her a foil-wrapped sandwich and poured coffee from a thermos into a paper cup. "Cream?"

She shook her head and took the warm cup eagerly into her cold hands. The temperature had begun to drop as evening approached, and even in her jacket, she was beginning to feel the difference. The coffee was hot, strong, and rich, and she leaned back against the side of the gondola and sighed with contentment.

She munched happily on the ham and cheese sandwich he handed her and asked, "Did you finish your puzzle?"

He shook his head. "Not yet. But I think I've found the key." He shrugged. "Once you've done that, it's all downhill. I'll have it completely deciphered by tomorrow." He took a sip of coffee. "Most of the challenge is over after you've found the key." In the fading light his eyes were oddly weary. Weary and a little lonely.

Kelly felt a shiver run through her, and she dropped her eyes to the cup in her hand. "That's too bad," she said with forced lightness. "You'll just have to find something else to amuse you, won't you?" She noticed that he had not taken a sandwich himself. "You're not eating. Aren't you hungry?"

He shook his head. "I had a sandwich earlier while you were sleeping." His blue eyes were twinkling now. "I felt the need of something to occupy my attention while I was watching you wriggle and thrash about. Did you know that you make the sexiest little grunts imaginable while you're sleeping?"

She fixed a baleful eye on him. "Is that a kind way of telling me that I snore?" she asked, as she took the last bite of sandwich and crumpled the foil into a silver ball. "It's very rude to watch someone when they're sleeping."

He grinned. "I didn't say that you snored. It's more like a satisfied little purr. I found it very erotic." He drained his cup and crushed it idly. "But you're quite right. I shouldn't have invaded your privacy when you were at your most defenseless." He smiled again. "Suppose that I promise to return the favor at the earliest opportunity?"

Kelly's lips curved in a reluctant smile. "You're completely impossible, Nick O'Brien," she said, shaking her head reprovingly. "You must be really bored to bother using that lethal charm on me. I know that I'm the only woman available, but I'm certainly no Maria Dominguez."

A frown darkened his face, and he impatiently tossed his crushed cup back into the hamper. "You seem to be obsessed with the thought of that woman," he said curtly. "I told you she wasn't important."

"I'm very well aware of that," Kelly said quietly. "But then I doubt that any woman is important to you for very long." She finished the last of her coffee and carefully set the cup on the floor beside her. "I'd be a fool not to realize that after compiling a dossier on you that would have made Casanova blush."

"Damn your dossier!" O'Brien said with sudden roughness. He closed the hamper with a sharp snap and pushed it aside. "That has nothing to do with us!"

"No?" Kelly raised an eyebrow. "Perhaps I find the idea of being a statistic in your little black book a trifle distasteful, Nick. I don't think my ego would permit it."

O'Brien's lips twisted cynically. "No, I can see that you'd have a problem. I'd forgotten you're used to having your lovers dancing on your string. You like to be the one who loves them and leaves them."

"That's not true," Kelly protested hotly. "You may have time for those cute little games, but I certainly don't. I happen to be quite serious about my work."

"You'll forgive my skepticism, but I've only known you one day, and I've already encountered two of your current flames. Hell, you wouldn't be here at all if I hadn't decided that I didn't like the terms of that wager your Don Juan of a boss offered you! I'd say that we're pretty well matched as far as notches on the bedposts are concerned."

Mac, a Don Juan? That was as ridiculous as his assumption about her past. "You're rather prone to jumping to conclusions, aren't you?" She lifted her chin haughtily. "I suggest that we drop the subject. The entire discussion is irrelevant anyway. We both know that the only reason you brought me along was because I blackmailed you into it."

He laughed mirthlessly. "The hell you did, sweetheart. For your information, the government boys came begging to O'Brien Computers to receive one of the first shipments of the new models off the assembly line. There's no way they would have cancelled that order because of my affair with Maria."

Her green eyes widened incredulously. "Then why did you let me think that I'd manipulated you into agreeing? Why am I here now?"

He frowned. "Damned if I know," he growled, his eyes flickering with anger and another emotion that caused a sudden surge of heat to course through her. "I sure as hell can do without the brand of voltage you generate in me, Goldilocks. From the moment that I saw you, I wanted to drag you off to bed and keep you there for a week. You turn me on more than any woman I've ever met." His voice roughened sharply. "If that was all there was to it, I'd be a happy man right now, and I can assure you that you'd be a very satisfied lady. But that's not all, damn it. You arouse emotions in me that disturb the devil out of me. I'm not used to feeling protective and possessive and murderously jealous all at the same time. I liked my life very well as it was before the appearance of one small green-eyed blond!"

"Well, I'm sure it's only a temporary aberration. You'll probably not remember my name next week." Why was she feeling so hurt at O'Brien's bluntness? He was only stating what she'd told herself only a few hours ago. She blinked rapidly and swallowed to relieve the aching tightness in her throat. She would not cry, damn it.

She leaped to her feet and turned her back on O'Brien to gaze blindly out at the sunset. At any other time she would have been struck breathless at the incredible beauty of the fiery crimson rays that turned the clouds below and around her into a misty pink world paved with corridors of gold. The hills and valleys of the earth below them were gowned in the cool, rich violet of early evening, but here in the clouds there was only vibrant, singing color. Kelly noticed the glorious phenomenon almost absently as she struggled to repress the thought of O'Brien's explosive rejection.

"I wish I could be as confident regarding that as you are, Goldilocks." She had not heard his silent approach, but he was suddenly standing behind her. He was so close that she could feel the heat emanating from his body, and his breath stirred the curls about her ear as he spoke. "But you forget that I'm cursed with total recall. You just might turn out to be a permanent affliction."

Kelly could feel the breath catch in her throat as his lips brushed the curve of her ear. She could feel the electric vitality of his hard, muscular body as he shifted forward, pressing her into the side of the gondola. His arms slid around her slim waist. "Since we both agree that a serious relationship is the last thing that we want, I think we owe it to each other to dissipate the mystique, don't you?" he asked huskily, his lips moving to her nape and brushing light, teasing kisses beneath the curly, sun-streaked ringlets.

"I—I don't know what you mean," she faltered, instinctively bending her head to receive those deliciously gentle kisses.

He chuckled. "Yes, you do," he said softly. "I can feel you tremble in my arms. You want it just as much as I do, sweetheart, and God knows I've been in a fever for you since you barged into my apartment yesterday afternoon." His hands moved up the front of her jacket and found the zipper at the collar. With one swift stroke the jacket was open, and his hands closed on her high, firm breasts.

"No, you're wrong!" she cried desperately. His hands were warm through the thin cotton of her shirt, and even as she spoke the words of rejection, she felt herself succumbing to the slow, gentle kneading motion. "I don't want this," she said weakly.

"I love these bouncy little curls of yours," he whispered burying his lips in her hair. "Your hair is like silky, golden fleece. I bet those curls would wind themselves around my finger and cling like a lover's embrace if I buried my hands in them. Would they do that, Kelly?"

"Yes," she gasped, feeling as if her bones were melting as his hands continued their sensual massage of her breasts. "No!" She shook her head. "I don't know. I wish you'd stop that." She wondered bewilderedly why she wasn't struggling to be released.

"You don't like it?" he asked. "I guess I'll have to find something you do like, sweetheart." Suddenly he stepped back and turned her into his embrace, his arms binding her soft curves to his lean, hard body. "I like this better, too," he said hoarsely. "God, you're so soft and sweet against me. See how beautifully you fit in my arms?"

She did see, she thought dreamily. It seemed so unbelievably right to be so close to him. He was right, their bodies did flow together. His head bent toward her lips with the infinite slowness one would use in tempting a frightened bird to one's hand, and when they covered her own, she found that the merging was as inevitably right as the fit of their bodies.

O'Brien took his time with the leisurely expertise he would have employed in the tasting of a fine wine. He brushed and nibbled at her lips before taking them in a long, lingering kiss of dizzying sweetness.

"God, wasn't that terrific, love?" Nick murmured hoarsely. He was as breathless as she, the pulse beating rapidly in the hollow of his throat. "It's going to be fantastic between us." Without waiting for her reply, his lips compulsively moved back to hers. "Sweet, so sweet. Open your lips, I want to taste every bit of you, sweetheart."

Oh, and she wanted to taste all of him, too, she found. Her mouth parted eagerly to invite his tongue to explore, and her own tentative probing proved almost more than she could stand. Everything about him was clean and hot and wonderfully, solidly male. She felt as if she were being absorbed in him. Her lips, tongue, and every nerve in her body responded to the molten challenge he was offering.

She didn't know at what point they sank to their knees on the floor of the gondola or when he pulled her across his lap to cradle her in his arms. She was too absorbed in the silky feel of his dark hair between her fingers and the rapid throb of his heart against her breast. His breathing was shallow, and he was whispering erotic praise between their passionate kisses. She could feel the muscles of his thighs tense and harden beneath her, and she was vaguely conscious of his tremendous arousal. His blue eyes were blazing brilliantly in a face taut with desire. The mouth that was driving her weak with need was beautifully soft and sensual.

Then his hands were moving frantically at the buttons of her olive blouse and the front closure of her bra beneath it. He pushed the restricting material aside impatiently and looked down at her full, high breasts. "Damn, you're lovely," he said huskily, his chest moving almost painfully with the force of his breathing. His palms reached out to cup her breasts tenderly. "I was almost hoping you wouldn't be this perfect. I didn't want to know how delicious you would feel in my hands." He closed his eyes, his sensitive fingertips caressing and kneading her silky softness in erotic braille.

It was too much. Kelly felt as if each gentle stroking touch were leaving a trail of fire in its wake. Those strong, graceful hands were arousing her to a wild need that she had never known before. Her entire body was responding to that teasing manipulation as if she were a puppet and he were pulling the strings. His maddening fingers rubbed gently at a button-hard nipple, and a shudder of pure desire shook her.

He looked down at her in quick concern. His aquamarine eyes were almost glazed with need as they gazed down at the engorged result of his love play. "You're cold. Let me warm you," he said thickly. His hands left her for a moment to quickly unzip his jacket and unbutton his shirt. Then she was gathered securely against his hair-roughened chest.

Cold? She'd never been less cold in her life, she thought feverishly. Her temperature continued to climb as he began to undulate her body lazily against his own, the dark hair of his chest prickling and teasing her breasts until her breath was coming in little gasps and her hands were digging desperately into his shoulders as if to hold on before she was swept away in the wake of this hot whirlpool of sensation.

"Ah, you like that," Nick murmured. "So do I, love. You're like soft, warm velvet except for those lovely little nipples. They're like crisp taffeta." He drew a deep, shuddering breath. "They're driving me absolutely insane."

And what did he think he was doing to her? she thought wildly. She was experiencing a hot, throbbing ache in her loins, and she felt dizzy and weak. The touch of his warm hardness was almost as painful as the thought of doing without it.

"Nick," she gasped, her lips burying themselves in

the hollow between his shoulder and his throat. "Nick, I can't stand this."

"Neither can I." He groaned. "I've got to have more of you, Kelly. I want to see all of you and touch every inch of you. I feel as if I could devour you and still never satisfy my hunger."

With one swift movement, he shifted her off his lap so that she was lying on the floor of the small gondola. He was beside her immediately, lying facing her, his arms wrapped loosely around her while he covered her face and throat with swift kisses.

"This is crazy." Kelly moaned, even as her small hands ran lovingly up the powerfully sculptured muscles of his chest to slide around his shoulders and caress his neck. "It's all happening too fast, Nick."

His hands were busy unfastening her belt, and he looked up and grinned. "If I don't get you out of these clothes, it may not be fast enough," he said ruefully. "Lord, I'm wild for you, Kelly." He had managed to unfasten the zipper on her jeans, and one warm hand slid beneath the material to caress the softness of her belly. "Velvet again," he said thickly. Then as his hand wandered further, "And my lovely golden fleece."

Kelly inhaled sharply and opened her lips to utter a weak protest, but his lips were covering hers again, and she forgot what she was going to say. Then his skillful hands were on her breasts once more, and his lips moved down to caress the sensitive nipples. He began teasing them with the tip of his tongue. Her body jerked and then arched as if she had been stroked with electricity.

Nick gave her flushed, dreamy face a keen, appraising glance. "Your breasts are so beautifully responsive," he said hoarsely. "I'll remember that, sweetheart. I want to make you just as wild as you're driving me." He lowered his head and pulled gently with his teeth at one engorged nipple.

What did he want to do to her? she thought

desperately. She was already going out of her mind with the sensations that he was creating in every nerve of her body. She was shaking, and she felt so weak that she doubted if she could move a muscle except at his urging. He seemed to be controlling not only her physical responses but the surroundings around them. He had narrowed the world down until it contained only his intent, dark face and the flaming sky above them.

Flaming?

"Oh, my God!" Her voice was hoarse with terror. "We're on fire!"

"That's what I've been trying to tell you." Nick said chuckling, his eyes on the taut pink bud he was caressing.

"No!" she cried frantically. "Nick, we're really on fire. The balloon's on fire!"

He lifted his head swiftly to the nylon mushroom above them and the flame that was licking at the base of the chute. He uttered a string of obscenities before sitting bolt upright and rapidly buttoning his shirt.

"What can we do?" Kelly asked frantically. "Can we put it out?"

"Not a chance," he said tersely. He stood up and went quickly to the pile of supplies and blankets beside the burners. "In about two minutes that canopy is going to be completely engulfed in flames, and we'll drop like a stone. We'll have to jump." He had retrieved a bright orange parachute pack and was strapping it on swiftly. "And it's going to take me that long to get into this thing."

"Jump?" Kelly repeated, sitting up dazedly. "I don't even know how to use a parachute."

His lips curved wryly. "I'm afraid any skills you might have would be useless, anyway. I wasn't expecting a passenger, so there's only one parachute."

"Only one . . ." she said faintly, her eyes widening.

"Don't worry," he said, his expression terse. "I'll take care of you."

"Don't worry!" she almost shouted, as she jumped to her feet. "I'm seventeen thousand feet above the ground in a balloon that's about to go up in flames, and I don't have a parachute! And you tell me not to worry?"

"Well, a little concern might not be out of place," he admitted. "We'll just use my parachute. Now, get dressed."

In her shock she had totally forgotten that her blouse was completely opened. She turned away from him and hastily put her clothes in order.

"Make sure your belt is tightly fastened," he said.

Was the man completely mad? she wondered. Nevertheless, she did what he told her.

He had the parachute on now, and he quickly rummaged through the supplies as she zipped up her jacket. "Good thing I had this with me," he said, holding up a small device.

A mountaineering snap link, she thought dazedly. "Will it work?" she asked as he stooped slightly and attached the link to her belt, then to the harness of the parachute, binding them very close together.

"Sure, it will," he said, straightening and simultaneously lifting her. "Now, wrap your legs around me and grab on to the front of the harness—tight. Much as I'd like to, I won't be able to hold on to you. I'll be too busy with the parachute."

As she held tightly to the harness front, her legs wrapped around him, he hoisted them both up onto the rim of the basket, then swung his legs to the outside of the gondola.

Kelly shivered in fear. She was jumping out of a balloon with only a snap link and her own strong arms to rely on.

Nick looked down at her face, his expression suddenly serious. "You're not really frightened, are you?"

he asked quietly. "You know that I wouldn't let anything hurt you."

She raised her eyes to meet his grave, steady gaze, and suddenly her fear was gone. She knew that she'd never be safer than when she was with this eccentric, dynamic man. "No, I'm not afraid," she said softly, her eyes alight with warm trust and a hint of wry humor. "I'm just ruing the day that I decided to blackmail Superman. I don't think I'm cut out for flying without wings."

"Don't knock it until you try it, Lois," he said. There was a reckless smile on his face. "This isn't the way I wanted to send you soaring, love, but it will have to do."

He gave her a quick kiss, then suddenly he lunged forward, sending them both into space.

Four

The jar as they hit the earth was bone shaking even though O'Brien managed to land on his feet before rolling over. He attempted to absorb most of the impact with his own body. As quickly as he could, he released the snap link. The orange parachute enveloped them, and it was a moment before O'Brien could rid himself of the harness and thrust the layers of cloth impatiently away from them.

"Okay?" he asked quietly.

She nodded a trifle breathlessly and sat up. "I'll have a few bruises tomorrow," she said, as she rubbed the small of her back gingerly. "But nothing that I can't handle."

"I'm beginning to believe that there's very little you can't handle, Kelly McKenna." Nick stood up and helped her to her feet. "I just may decide to take you on all my skydiving jaunts."

"Please don't," she said, running a hand through her tumbled golden curls. "Once was enough, thank you." She peered around her anxiously. The terrain around them was rough and rocky, and they seemed to be on an incline. "You wouldn't know where we are by any chance?"

He shrugged. "Not exactly. Somewhere in the hill country near the base of the Sierra Madre I would guess." He bent down and began to gather up and fold the chute. "Far from any sign of civilization at any rate."

Kelly automatically began to help him with the chute, her eyes fixed on his calm face. "Charming," she said. "And how are we to make our way back to said civilization?"

"We'll manage," he said carelessly. "But after I get this chute repacked, I think we'd better worry about finding some sort of shelter for the night. The temperature can drop pretty sharply in the hills at night."

"Perhaps you can give me a crash course on body temperature control," Kelly said flippantly, buttoning the tab collar at the throat of her jacket. It was already quite cool.

"Sorry, sweetheart, it doesn't work that way." He chuckled. "Don't worry, I'll keep you warm."

She had no doubt that he could at that, she thought. She could not deny the strong sexual chemistry that existed between them, but it didn't change her reasons for not wanting any kind of relationship with O'Brien. She'd be a fool to let herself become involved in an affair that would only mean pain. She would just have to guard carefully against any further sexual encounters with Nick O'Brien. Which might not be all that easy, she thought. Nick had been just as lost in that haze of wild passion as she, and he was obviously used to getting exactly what he wanted from women. It was extremely unlikely that he would give up any plans he might have for seducing her now that he'd had a taste of how wildly they could please each other. She would just have to think of some way to discourage him and still hold on to her own control. It would be a task, she thought, that just might prove more dangerous than that jump out of the balloon.

Once the chute was repacked, Nick slung it over his shoulder. "Let's go," he said. Taking her small hand in his, he propelled her briskly down the incline toward the foothills.

Kelly found it oddly companionable walking hand in hand down the rock-strewn hill through the gathering darkness. Strange that she experienced this total unconcern regarding the dilemma that they were in. She felt almost lighthearted, as if she were starting out on a brave new adventure, and she knew that her serenity was due to the man beside her. It was difficult to be frightened or worried when he was so assured and competent. Perhaps that comparison that she had drawn with Superman wasn't so far off the mark, she thought.

They had reached the bottom of the hill, and Nick's pace quickened as he moved purposefully toward a clearing sheltered by a sparse growth of surrounding cottonwoods. Darkness had fallen fully now, and the clearing looked oddly desolate and menacing in the shadowy guardianship of the trees.

O'Brien took off the parachute pack when they reached the clearing and dropped it on the ground. "Stay here," he ordered. "I'll go gather some wood and build a fire."

"I'll go with you and help," Kelly said in a determined tone. She might as well start out as she meant to continue. O'Brien needn't think that he was going to treat her like some helpless little clinging vine. She would carry her full share of the work and responsibility in this situation.

In the darkness she couldn't see the expression on O'Brien's face, but his voice was rich with amusement. "I think I detect the signs of women's lib surfacing. All right, Goldilocks, I wouldn't dream of suppressing that independent spirit."

It appeared that he meant exactly what he said. He not only let her help gather wood and carry it back to the clearing, but also set her the task of finding stones to bank the flames while he busied himself with the actual building of the fire. When she had finished encircling the burning wood with several large, flat stones, she sank down beside it and sighed in contentment.

She watched O'Brien lithely move about, first stacking their reserves of wood in a readily accessible pile near them, and then unpacking the parachute and spreading it on the ground before the fire.

When he'd finished, he sat down on the brilliant nylon and patted the place beside him. "Come over here and join me, Goldilocks, and we'll fire-gaze together," he invited.

"Fire-gaze?" she asked, getting up and moving slowly to join him on the chute. "I've heard of star-gazing but never fire-gazing."

"Fire-gazing is much more interesting," he said, as he put an arm about her shoulders and pulled her close. "You can almost hypnotize yourself into seeing any shape or image you want to see."

"Like seeing a camel in a bank of clouds?" Kelly asked, her green eyes sparkling.

He shook his head reprovingly. "You're wandering into an entirely different field," he said sternly. "Now cease your flippancy and apply yourself, woman."

"Yes, sir!" she said meekly, and settled herself more comfortably in the curve of his arm. She had an idea that obeying Nick's invitation to join him was going to prove a serious mistake, but for the moment she was too content to move.

She soon found that Nick was right about the magnetic effect of gazing into the fire. She was in a state of drowsy bemusement sometime later when Nick stirred himself to get up and throw more wood on the fire. She hadn't been aware of Nick's hand toying idly with her curls, but she missed the feel of those lazily caressing fingers when he moved away. She shook her head as if to clear it. She was already feeling cold and lonely without his sheltering arm, and she knew that this sort of dependence was extremely dangerous.

When Nick returned to his place beside her, she shifted a discreet distance away and turned to face him. "Perhaps we should start trying to find our way out of these hills tonight," she suggested nervously. "We don't have any food or water, and there's no telling how long it will take us to find help."

O'Brien's blue eyes narrowed in thoughtful appraisal at her change in attitude. "Tomorrow will be soon enough," he said slowly. "We can't do much but stumble around in the dark until we get our bearings. Once it's light, I'll set about canvassing the area for water and food to supply us for our hike. We'll be in much better shape after a good night's sleep. And speaking of sleep," he continued silkily, "I think it's time we retired, sweetheart."

Before she could reply, he had pushed her gently back on the nylon chute and was bending over her, laughing down into her startled face. "Shall I help you undress?" he asked politely. Then as she shook her head firmly and opened her lips to protest, he sighed. "It's just as well. I might be a bit too enthusiastic getting you out of your clothes, and they're the only ones you have. For the last hour I've been wondering how cream velvet and golden fleece would look against this silky orange chute."

Kelly could feel that odd weakness beginning to affect her limbs at the picture his words invoked. She was beginning to quiver inside with that same hot sensation she had known such a short time before.

"No!" she said, pushing him away with a force that surprised both of them. She sat upright and scrambled away from him. "No, it's not going to be that way, Nick. I'm not going to be one of your one-night stands. It was all a mistake."

His expression hardened. "The hell it was," he said roughly. "It was fantastic, and you know it. I've been going out of my mind wanting you since before we jumped out of that balloon, and I'm not letting you cheat us both because of some crazy prejudice you have against my lurid past." His lips curved in a mocking smile. "I think you'll have to admit that in less than five minutes I can make you forget all about your precious scruples."

Kelly bit her lip uncertainly as she gazed into his dark, ruthless face. How could she deny what they both knew was true? Yet she must find some way of discouraging him from instigating that threatened assault on her senses. Her mind searched wildly for an answer. The obvious solution was to make him so angry with her that he would forget about the overwhelming physical attraction between them. The question was how that was going to be accomplished. She knew that insults would have no effect on Nick; he was the most confident, self-assured individual she had ever known.

"You might make me want you, but it wouldn't change my mind," she said stubbornly. "I won't sleep with you, Nick."

For a moment she thought the flicker behind Nick's cool stare was the anger that she was looking for, but it was quickly masked by a sardonic expression. "Why should I be the only one left out?" he asked silkily. "Do you compile a dossier on all your men before deciding which one to take to your bed?" His lips thinned bitterly. "You were even willing to jump into bed with that damn editor if you'd lost your bet. Why shouldn't I be allowed the same privileges as the rest of your male harem?"

Her eyes widened at his words. For a moment she did not even make the connection; then she felt a wild urge to laugh aloud. True, she had not told Nick the reason for the wager. She started to explain when she noticed the hard, tight line of Nick's jaw and the glaring expression in his eyes. He was jealous! He had told her that he was possessive of her, but she had not believed him. Yet, if he was a bit jealous, she might be able to use it to her advantage.

"It's funny that you mentioned a harem," she said lightly. "We both seem to have a passion for variety. Of course, you're older and have more experience than I, but as I was reading over your dossier, I felt a real sense of kinship with you." She lowered her eyes to the fire, her long lashes veiling her gleaming jade eyes. "Though it really wasn't fair of me to so familiarize myself with your affairs when you knew nothing about mine." She lifted her gaze to meet his eyes with what she hoped was a look of complete innocence. "Would you like me to tell you about my first lover?"

"No, I would not," Nick said, between clenched teeth. She noticed with satisfaction that a muscle twitched in his lean cheek.

"You're right," she returned earnestly. "First affairs are so callow that they're not a bit interesting in retrospect. It's only after you gain more experience and sophistication that you can really appreciate the nuances of a relationship. Don't you find that true, Nick?"

"I'd rather not discuss it," he said coldly, reaching over to stoke the fire with a stick.

"Of course, you wouldn't." Kelly rocked back on her heels and demurely linked her hands together in front of her. "Why should you reveal any more of yourself to me, when I've not been equally generous?" She smiled at him with enchanting sweetness. "If we're going to become as intimate as you wish, you're entitled to my complete confidence. Would you like to know only who they were, or do you want to know what we actually did in bed?"

"Kelly!" The word was uttered in such a savage tone that it momentarily intimidated her.

She recovered swiftly, however. "I suppose I should

start with Raoul," she said, tilting her head considingly. "He was really the first man who taught me anything about what lovemaking should mean to a woman." Her lips curved in a dreamy smile. "He worked at the French embassy in Algiers. Then there was Pedro Salazar, a bullfighter in Madrid. He was really magnificent, so strong and graceful. He had the most divine thrust." She looked up at him limpidly. "I mean his sword thrust, of course."

"Of course," Nick repeated savagely. His bronzed face was set in grim lines, his half-closed eyes fixed on the flames.

"I'll skip the less important ones," Kelly went on. "But I really think you should hear about Ian Cartwright. He was a game warden in Nigeria, and he taught me the most interesting—"

"No!" Nick shouted, and the face he turned to her was corroded with rage and passion. "Damn you, shut up!" His hands were on her shoulders, and he was shaking her with such force that she suspected she'd have bruises the next day. "What the hell are you trying to do to me?" he rasped. "I don't know whether I'm going to strangle you or rape you, but you can damn well believe it's going to be something violent!"

"Nick, don't," Kelly whispered, her face suddenly so pale that her eyes were like emeralds in its whiteness. "I didn't mean—"

"I know exactly what you meant to do. You wanted to get a little of your own back by roasting me over the flames." His blue eyes were like daggers boring into hers. "Well, you'll be glad to know that you succeeded. I hope it was worth it to you, because I don't think you're going to like the result of your little game of true confessions." His hand moved up to tangle in her curls and draw her head back. "I'm never going to let you out of my sight from now on, and if you so much as look at another man, I'll kill him!" The words were bullet hard and held a chilling sincerity.

"Nick—" Kelly said falteringly, "I have to tell—"

"You've told me enough," he said tersely, releasing her and backing away, his expression stormy. "And I don't want to hear another word out of you, or, so help me God, I'll break your little neck."

"But I only—"

"Kelly, if I have to warn you again, it won't be with words," he growled menacingly. He straightened the chute on the ground and lay down on the other side of it. Then he propped himself up on one elbow. "I'm just aching to get my hands on you one way or the other, so if I were you, I wouldn't tempt me. Now come and lie down."

She looked away unhappily. "I think I'll stay up for a while."

"Kelly!" His tone was commanding.

"Oh, very well," she said crossly, as she stretched out gingerly as far from Nick as the chute permitted.

"Over here, Kelly," Nick ordered. "You needn't be afraid that I'll hurt you. I may be angry, but I have no intention of using you roughly."

"I'm quite comfortable here," Kelly protested uneasily, turning her back on him. Who could have known that Nick would explode like that. He had frightened her.

"Nevertheless, you'll come over here. You have a right to be wary of me. At the moment, I'm using all my willpower just to keep myself under control. I have no intention of making love to you. I'm so angry that I'm afraid I'd hurt you. But you'll sleep in my arms tonight and every night from now on. Do you understand?"

She nodded silently and then obediently scooted close to him to be enfolded in his warm, strong embrace. Why was she being so meek and docile? It must be weariness and the shock of that violent, emotional outpouring from Nick that made her want only to relax and avoid any further arguments.

"That's the first intelligent thing you've done in the past hour," he said. He turned and shifted her body so that her back was to him and her body fitted into his spoon fashion; his arms formed a warm, secure stronghold around her. "All hell would have broken loose if you'd fought me on this." He reached over her and pulled the other edge of the nylon chute over both of them as a blanket.

"I don't think this is very good idea," Kelly ventured uncertainly. His hard, tense frame was a burning brand against her, and she could feel how aroused he was. "How can we get to sleep like this?"

"We probably won't," he said curtly, his breath blowing the golden ringlets at her ear. "We'll probably both lie here all night aching and feverish." He laughed mirthlessly. "I'm damned sure that I won't get any rest!"

"Then let me go back where I was," she whispered reasonably. "It will be better for both of us."

His arms tightened possessively around her. "Frankly, at the moment I don't give a damn what's best for us. The only thing that's important right now is teaching you that, no matter how many men you've had in the past, it's only my arms you'll sleep in from now on."

"Until you get tired of me," Kelly said tartly.

She could feel the deep, ragged breath he took. "Kelly," he said softly, "shut up!"

The first thing she saw when she opened her eyes early in the morning was the tip of a dusty, scuffed brown boot some six inches from her face. The second was a butt of a rifle in the dust beside that boot!

Startled, she jumped upright and felt Nick's cautioning hand on her shoulder. "Easy, Kelly," he said quietly. "It seems that we have visitors. Let me handle it."

Kelly felt a twinge of resentment at his words. He was doing it again. Pushing her under his protective wing as if she were completely ineffectual in a crisis. Then, as the sleep cleared from her eyes and she got a better look at the visitors, she let her breath out in a soundless whistle. Perhaps she'd let Nick have his way after all.

There were about twenty Mexican men in the clearing. Their hair was long and unkempt, several were bearded, and their sombreros, worn jeans, and colorful shirts were dusty and food stained. Each man carried a holstered pistol at his hip and a rifle in his hands. Altogether, they were as dangerous a looking lot as she'd ever seen. Several yards from the clearing, she could see four additional men standing guard over a number of dusty, wild-looking horses.

"Who are they?" Kelly whispered, leaning back against O'Brien's solid body.

"I was just about to find out." Tossing aside their nylon cover, he stood up. "And I don't think we'll be pleased with the answer."

As she hastily scrambled to her feet, she heard Nick speaking quickly in Spanish. Why had she not learned Spanish? she wondered desperately, looking anxiously from O'Brien's face to the blank, impassive faces of the Mexicans confronting them. Evidently he had asked to speak to their leader, for a slight, almost delicate-appearing man in a brilliant red shirt strolled forward to stand before O'Brien. The man had a wolfish grin on his bearded face. His answer was as terse and businesslike as O'Brien's question, but it evoked several chuckles from his men.

Kelly grabbed Nick's arm and whispered, "What did he say?"

To her annoyance he shrugged off her hand and deliberately stepped in front of her and spoke again.

His reply elicited an even bigger laugh than the Mexican's, and for the next five minutes there was a verbal interchange that sounded maddeningly casual to Kelly. When he turned to face her, she was steaming with impatience.

"It appears you attract trouble like a magnet, Goldilocks," he said softly. "These charming fellows seem to want to hold us for ransom."

"Ransom!" Kelly exclaimed, her mouth falling open. "You mean they're some kind of criminals?"

"Bandidos," he corrected. "It seems it's an old and honorable profession in these hills. Pedro Garcia, here, tells me that they're sure we're very fine birds to be plucked because no one but a rich, crazy gringo would think of sailing across Mexico in a balloon."

"Well, he's half right," Kelly muttered. "How did they know about the balloon?"

"They saw it fall 'like a flaming star from heaven,' " he quoted mockingly. "They rode out and located the wreckage and then started looking for us. They spotted our campfire about an hour ago."

"Well, what are we going to do?" she asked, running her hand through her curls. "We can't let them get away with this."

"*You* are going to do absolutely nothing," Nick said crisply. "I am going to negotiate and see what I can do about getting us out of this. I want you to stay out of this and keep a low profile. Have you got that, Goldilocks?"

She drew herself up indignantly, her jade eyes flashing. "Did it ever occur to you that I might be able to help? I'm not completely useless, you know. Perhaps I can persuade him to let us go."

He frowned. "You don't even speak the language. Stay out of it, Kelly."

"Then you can interpret," Kelly said stubbornly. "I'm going to talk to him." Before he could stop her, she stepped quickly around him and strode swiftly up to the bandit leader. Her heart was beating like a trip-hammer, and she could feel the familiar surge of excitement as she stopped before him and looked up into his narrow, dark face. She gave him an appealing smile, and to her relief, he returned the smile, though his was a trifle feral, she thought.

"Tell him that I'm a reporter for an important American magazine," she told O'Brien over her shoulder. "Tell him that I can make him as famous as Pancho Villa." As she spoke, she continued to smile up at Pedro Garcia entrancingly.

"Kelly." O'Brien's voice was menacing. "Get the hell away from him. Now!"

"Tell him," she insisted, fluttering her long lashes and increasing the voltage of the smile. "Everyone wants to see his name in print, particularly crooks. Look at all the books written by criminals in prison."

"Kelly, you idiot," O'Brien said tersely. "Do what I say!"

The bandit's smile widened to a beaming grin, and Kelly said excitedly, "I think we're making progress. Will you just—" She broke off, her eyes wide with shock, as the bandit's hand reached out and cupped her breast in his palm. Uttering a little cry, she stepped back. She heard the rest of the bandits break out in guffaws and O'Brien swear.

"I hope you're satisfied," O'Brien said savagely. His arm went around her and brought her swiftly into its protective circle. "I could throttle you!"

"I just wanted to help," she said defensively, moving closer to him. Pedro Garcia was laughing and gesturing toward her, trading comments with his cohorts, which they were all finding vastly entertaining.

"And instead, you just about got yourself raped," O'Brien bit out grimly. "Why do you think I wanted you to fade into the background, for God's sake? These men have never heard of your precious women's lib. They have only one use for a woman, and you're beautifully equipped for that."

"No wonder you're getting along with them so famously," she said tartly. "Your views are so similar."

"You'd better hope that I can convince them of that. From the remarks they're tossing around, you're still not out of hot water."

Kelly felt a shiver of fear run through her as she looked around the clearing at the men who were gazing at her in leering speculation. "I see what you mean," she said, moistening her lips nervously. "Do you think you can discourage them?"

"I'm going to do my damndest," he said tightly, his eyes darting warily about the clearing.

She nestled closer and turned her frightened gaze up to his hard, taut face. "Would it help if you told them that I was a virgin?" she whispered anxiously. "No one wants an inexperienced woman these days. They're out of fashion."

O'Brien's shocked gaze flew to her worried face, then he gave a mirthless laugh. "It might help at that. If they knew what an experienced little madam you are, they'd probably be standing in line for your favors."

"Will you stop joking?" she cried desperately, her green eyes suspiciously bright. "Damn it, I *am* a virgin, and I don't want my first experience to be a gang-bang."

His body stiffened as if he'd been struck by a bullet. He drew a deep breath. "And what about your magnificent bullfighter and that Nigerian game warden?" he asked carefully, his tone all the more menacing for its very control.

Kelly flushed, her gaze shifting away guiltily. "Well, I actually exaggerated a little last night," she told him sheepishly. "I knew that you really wouldn't want to become involved with me, either, once you had time to mull it over, so I did the only thing I could think of to keep us from making a terrible mistake." She peeped at him sidewise to see if he was as angry as she thought. He was. She continued in a rush, "Besides, you probably wouldn't have enjoyed it, anyway. A man of your experience would find a virgin staggeringly boring."

"Boring you're not," he said, enunciating each word carefully. "Your little 'exaggeration' almost caused me to do something we both would have regretted, and I assure you that lying beside you all night and aching to take you was far from dull."

She bristled indignantly. "That wasn't my fault. I did—"

"We'll discuss it later," he interrupted grimly. "Right now I've got to try to get you out of this mess." He removed his arm from around her and started toward the bandit leader. He turned to say harshly over his shoulder, "You needn't look so anxious. I'm not about to let any of these clowns rape you. It's *me* you've got to worry about."

The negotiations and discussions between O'Brien and the bandit leader took most of the day. Much to Kelly's disgust, she was left to sit by herself under a tree while Nick spent the day talking with Pedro and his cohorts. Nick seemed to be in no hurry at all and was as lazily relaxed as if he were at a bachelor stag party. By late afternoon, judging by the joking and back-slapping on both sides, he appeared to be on excellent terms with all of them. To Kelly's extreme irritation, he even spent the last few hours before sunset playing *cards* with them, for heaven's sake!

As darkness fell, the campfire was rebuilt, and meal preparations got underway. The appetizing smell of bacon and beans wafted to her along with that most delicious scent of all, fresh-brewed coffee. Her stomach was growling as the men sat down to eat. She had been sent a water canteen earlier in the day by the bandit leader, obviously at his buddy O'Brien's suggestion, Kelly thought crossly. But she'd been given nothing to eat, and it seemed that they had no intention of supplying her with any supper. O'Brien was certainly not so deprived, she noticed resentfully, as he took a second helping of beans and sat back down by Pedro Garcia. He could at least have sent her some coffee.

The meal was over, and some of the bandits had started unrolling bedrolls beside the fire when Nick finally stood up and stretched lazily. He murmured something to Pedro that evoked a loud guffaw, then stooped to fill a plate with beans from the iron pot hanging above the campfire. He filled a tin cup with coffee, picked up a spoon, and strolled leisurely over to where Kelly was sitting beneath the tree on the outskirts of the clearing.

He handed her the plate, spoon, and coffee, then silently dropped down beside her on the chute. He leaned back against the tree and watched her as she hungrily started to eat. "Sorry I couldn't get anything to you before," he said quietly. "It was a bit dicey for a while, and I didn't want to rock the boat by calling attention to you."

Kelly found that she was feeling much more understanding now that her hunger was being assuaged. The beans weren't bad either, a little hot perhaps. "For a while I wasn't certain if you were going to join their merry little band. You've certainly all gotten to be great chums." She took a swallow of coffee and made a face. It was as thick as syrup, and it was almost cold. It had smelled much better than it tasted.

"It might not be such a bad life at that," he said teasingly. "No pressures, plenty of freedom, and nothing to do but extort money from crazy, rich gringos."

"And did he extort money from this particular crazy, rich gringo?" she asked, as she finished the beans. She set the plate and spoon down.

"We came to a mutual agreement," he said, reaching over to wipe a bit of sauce from the corner of her mouth with his fingers. "He's taking my wallet, including all the cash and credit cards, and tomorrow he's taking us to the outskirts of Matzalea, a small village about fifteen miles from here."

"But that's wonderful!" she said excitedly. "How did you get him to agree to let us go?"

He grinned. "We played cards for it," he said. "You're not the only one who likes an occasional wager, Goldilocks."

"But what did you have to bet?" she asked curiously, as she took the last swallow of that terrible coffee and put the cup on the ground beside the plate.

O'Brien chuckled, his dark face alight with mischief. "You," he said simply. "You'll be flattered to know that he considered you a very valuable commodity, sweetheart."

"Me!" Kelly cried indignantly, her mouth agape. "You gambled over me?"

"Yep."

"And what if you'd lost?" she asked, her jade eyes flaming. "Nick O'Brien, that's the most unprincipled thing I've ever heard of!"

"Relax, Kelly." He reached out and tugged at a curl. "I knew that I wouldn't lose. I cheated."

Her eyes widened. "That's even worse! What if they'd caught you? There's no telling what they'd have done to us."

He shook his head. "There was no chance of that. I knew exactly what I was doing. About four years ago I spent a few months in Las Vegas and—"

"No," Kelly interrupted, holding up her hand. "I don't even want to hear it." She sighed resignedly. "I should have known that Pedro Garcia wouldn't stand a chance with Superman. But if you won the game, why was it a bit dicey?"

He shrugged. "Pedro was a trifle reluctant to keep to the exact terms of the bet. He wanted you to share his bedroll tonight before he let us go tomorrow."

"And how did you convince him to reconsider?" Kelly asked slowly. She was just beginning to realize what a debt of gratitude she owed Nick. Despite his casual air, there were tiny lines of strain about his mouth, and for the first time since she had met him, she noticed that his brilliant vitality was slightly dimmed. While she had been sitting here beneath her tree fuming and mentally castigating him, he had been using all his skill and charisma to effect their release. It had obviously been a very difficult day for him.

O'Brien closed his eyes wearily and leaned his dark head back against the trunk of the tree. "I merely told him that if he so much as laid a hand on you, I'd forcibly remove an exceptionally prized portion of his anatomy."

She gave an amused chuckle. "And what would you have done if he'd called your bluff?"

His lids flickered open, and his eyes were glacier hard. "I would have done it," he said simply, and Kelly knew that he meant it.

She gave a little shiver. "Well, then it's a good thing he backed down," she said with forced lightness. "In case you hadn't noticed, we're slightly outnumbered."

"I noticed," he said laconically. He stood up and picked up her cup, plate, and spoon. "I'll see if I can't trade these for another blanket. It may not be as warm here as it would be closer to the campfire, but I'd just as soon keep you out of view in case Pedro has second thoughts."

Kelly watched him as he strode quickly over to the campfire and disposed of the plate, cup, and spoon. He spoke briefly to the bandit leader, who was almost asleep, and then picked up a gray- and black-striped blanket. He turned and strolled toward her, tossing a casual "*buenas noches*" over his shoulder.

Nick threw the striped blanket on her lap and dropped down beside her on the nylon chute. "We'd better get some shut-eye," he said, yawning. He stretched lazily, his muscles rippling beneath the black cotton shirt. He had half unbuttoned the shirt earlier in the heat of the day, and Kelly found she was having problems keeping her eyes off his powerful bronzed chest with its thatch of springy dark hair. "The trip to the village will be quite a walk, and I doubt if Pedro will put a horse at our disposal."

"You could always play cards for it," Kelly suggested, grinning.

He stripped off his shirt and folded it in a roll, then picked up his jacket and duplicated the action. He put both under his head and stretched out, sighing wearily. It seemed the most natural thing in the world to watch Nick as he prepared for the night, Kelly mused. Who would have dreamed that she could feel so intimate with any man after such a short time, much less someone as complicated and sophisticated as Nick? Yet, it wasn't so strange when she really thought about it. They had experienced more emotions and trying times together in the past forty-eight hours than another couple might in a year of courtship. Courtship? What an old-fashioned term for the passionate affair that Nick wanted to initiate, Kelly thought wryly. He wanted none of the graceful rituals that led to a permanent relationship, and she must accept that.

"You won't need your jacket with this blanket for cover," Nick said. "Take it off and use it for a pillow." He watched her as she unzipped the jacket, took it off, and folded it carefully. Then as she would have placed it on the other side of their nylon ground cover, he reached out and dragged it a few inches from his own. "I thought we'd settled that last night." He held out his arms imperiously. "Come here."

For a moment she was tempted to defy him on general principles. Then, noticing the weariness in his face, she felt a strange tenderness. He had earned his rest tonight, she thought, and she wasn't about to argue with him on such a trivial matter. She quietly curled up beside him with her back to him as she had the previous night. She felt his arms slide around her, drawing her closer to his warmth. He pulled the gray-striped blanket over both of them, tucking it under her chin, and then nuzzled his face in the soft curls at her nape. "Your hair smells like wood smoke and lemon," he said softly. "It's delicious. You should patent it."

She could feel the tempo of her heart increase as his lips brushed gently at the sensitive hollow beneath the silky ringlets.

"I don't think it would sell," she said faintly. "Not everyone is as discriminating as you. Most people prefer Chanel or Dior."

"Philistines," he said, his lips nibbling gently at her ear. "Your scent is much more erotic. It brings back tribal memories of cavemen seducing their women in front of a primitive campfire."

"I don't think it was seduction," Kelly gasped, as he pulled her back even closer against him. She could feel the virile heat of his naked chest through the thin cotton of her shirt. "I don't think they possessed that degree of subtlety."

He chuckled, and they were so close she could feel the vibrations of the muscles of his chest. "I thought a more delicate euphemism was called for under the circumstances," he said teasingly. "I wouldn't want to sully the ears of someone in your untouched state."

"You're not angry with me about that anymore?" she asked, trying to turn around to face him. "I wouldn't have lied to you if I hadn't thought it absolutely necessary."

He prevented her from moving by the simple means of tightening his arms until they were like warm bands of steel around her. "Lie still," he ordered. "That wriggling drives me out of my mind, and I've got to keep my cool tonight." As she obediently quieted, his arms loosened a bit, and he answered. "I'm not angry. Though, if you ever lie to me again, I just may do something violent." He drew a deep breath and buried his face in her hair again. "Once I thought about it, I found that I liked the idea of being your first lover so much that I didn't give a damn about your 'exaggerations'! I guess you've noticed that I'm a bit possessive of you?"

"I've noticed," Kelly said dryly, thinking of his threat to the bandit leader.

"Very uncivilized of me. But no more uncivilized than your virginity, sweetheart. How did I get so lucky?"

"You're very sure of yourself!" At his answering chuckle, she added crossly, "It's really none of your business, but I guess I do owe you something for those whoppers I told you. I suppose I was too busy with my career to get involved to that extent. I never saw what all the shouting was about." Not before the appearance of one Nick O'Brien. "I guess that makes me even more of a freak in your opinion," she finished belligerently.

"An enchanting freak," he agreed huskily, as his hands moved up to the buttons of her blouse. "I can hardly wait to normalize you, love." His hands were rapidly unbuttoning her blouse. "I wish to hell I could do it right here and now." His hand deftly freed the front catch of her bra.

"Nick, no!" Kelly whispered, her body tensing with shock as she glanced wildly at the slumbering men in the clearing. "You can't."

"I'm well aware of that," he said, his hands gently massaging her silky midriff. "Don't worry, Kelly. I'm not about to ravish you in a fit of lust for your nubile young body. I'll wait until I can make it good for you. I'm afraid that this damn weariness and our possible audience would preclude that tonight." His lips were at her ear again, and his breath was warm and gentle on her skin. "I just want to touch you. I want to hold you through the night and wake up with your lovely breasts in my hands. Will you let me do that?"

"I don't think it's a very good idea," Kelly said breathlessly. The idea may not have been either safe or reasonable in view of her determination not to have an affair with him, but it was wildly appealing.

"It's a *very* good idea. You'll see, sweetheart," Nick whispered. "You'll like my hands on you."

His warm gentleness was dizzyingly sweet as his hands left her midriff to caress her breasts tenderly. He was wrong. She *loved* his hands on her. For endless moments his hands explored the valley between her breasts, her nipples, and the creamy mounds. Then they moved up to her shoulders and her throat. Her upper arms, the hollow of her spine, her belly all received his concentrated tactile attention. When his hands returned reluctantly to her midriff, she felt as if he must know every curve and valley of her body more thoroughly than she did herself.

"I think that's enough for tonight," he said, his breathing a trifle shallow. "I'll have to save the rest for the next time, sweetheart. All my good intentions are on the verge of going down the drain." He pressed a quick kiss on the curve of her throat. "God, you're a lovely thing to touch." He snuggled close to her, his hands moving up to cup her breasts. "Go to sleep, Goldilocks. It may be some time before I can relax enough to join you."

Kelly almost laughed out loud. Couldn't he feel the crazy pounding of her heart beneath his hands? His explorations had not been meant to seduce her, she knew. But the gentle, probing curiosity of those long, sensitive fingers had made her wild with longing. For a moment or two she wouldn't have cared if he'd ignored their snoring companions and set about showing her more potent delights.

"Yes," she agreed huskily. "I'll go to sleep."

But it was a long time before she felt drowsy enough to ignore those warm, magnetic hands lightly cupping her breasts and fall into a restless slumber.

Five

Matzalea proved to be a tiny dusty village that looked as if it had been frozen in time over a century ago. It appeared to consist of just one main thoroughfare, which was unpaved. The street was bordered on each side by a straggle of adobe structures, which were dirty and generally seedy looking. The central attraction seemed to be the grimy chipped fountain in the center of the dusty road.

"It looks like an old Clint Eastwood spaghetti western," Kelly said, as she wiped the sweat off her brow with the sleeve of her jacket. "And where is everybody? It looks as if it's completely deserted."

"It's mid-afternoon, and that's siesta time in Mexico." Nick looked as hot as she felt, Kelly thought. Sweat had plastered his black shirt to his body so that it clung like a second skin, and his dark hair looked as damp as if he had been caught in a shower.

Shower. What a deliciously lovely thought that was. They'd been walking since just after dawn that morning—Nick had been correct in his assumption that the bandit leader would fail to supply them with horses. Consequently, they had trailed behind the outlaw band on foot, eating dust and slipping and sliding on the rough, rocky trails until Kelly wondered if she would actually make it to the village before collapsing from exhaustion. The coolness of the dawn had dissipated as the day progressed, and by noon they were both horribly hot and sweaty, as well as bone weary.

Matzalea may not have been an enchanted Brigadoon, but it had looked absolutely beautiful to her when they had reached the outskirts some ten minutes earlier. As soon as the village had come into view, the bandidos had left their captives to their own resources. Right up until the last moment, Kelly had thought that the bandit leader might change his mind about the agreement. She couldn't resist a sigh of relief when he'd laughingly called something back to Nick and then spurred his horse into a gallop, his men thundering at his heels.

"I'm so thirsty," Kelly said, wistfully looking at the fountain. "Do you suppose that water is sanitary?"

"I doubt it," Nick answered, his eyes searching the street keenly. "We'd better not risk it. It will be difficult enough getting out of here with no money or friends, without contracting Montezuma's Revenge."

"I guess you're right." Kelly sighed, rubbing the back of her neck tiredly. When she was a child, she had fallen ill with gastritis from drinking unboiled water in a little village in Ethiopia, and she had been so sick she had thought she might die. She certainly didn't want to risk that again. "What do you suggest we do then?"

"There's a tequilla bottle painted on a sign over the door of that building," Nick said, gesturing to a square adobe structure. "That's probably the local cantina. Let's see what we can do over there."

The interior of the cantina was small but blessedly

dim and cool after the cruel glare of the afternoon sun. The furniture consisted of a few tables and chairs and a crudely wrought wooden bar on the far side of the room. Evidently siesta time had taken its toll here also, for the room appeared to be deserted.

Nick deliberately closed the door behind them with a loud slam. "Let's hope that will bring someone running."

It brought someone, but she certainly wasn't running. The woman who appeared in the doorway beside the bar looked as if she'd never hurried in her life. She was in her middle thirties and decidedly plump. Her black, shiny hair was pushed back in a loose bun, and her dark eyes were tranquil. She was dressed in a yellow peasant blouse and a full, bright-orange skirt that made her generous hips look even plumper. She drifted toward them lethargically, her gaze as sleepy and uninterested as if strange gringos dropped in every day.

She did perk up, however, when she got a good look at Nick, Kelly noticed. The dark eyes actually lost their cowlike docility when he stepped forward flashing that charismatic grin, and spoke to her. He was evidently laying it on very thick indeed, for the señora was smiling, almost fawningly at him and answering with an eagerness that was practically vivacious.

"Her name is Carmen Rodriguez," Nick said, turning back to Kelly after a few minutes' conversation. "She's a widow and owns this cantina. She's going to let you stay here while I go and try to find some transport for us. It should be fairly safe. She says her customers don't usually start arriving until six."

Then he turned again and spoke rapidly to the woman. She gave him a glowing smile, nodded, turned, and disappeared through the door beside the bar. "She's going to boil you some water for drinking. Why don't you sit down? You look as if you're about to collapse."

There was a trace of anxiety in his voice that warmed her. "You're just as tired as I am," she said. "Probably much more tired. You half carried me over the roughest ground we traveled today."

He shook his head, his eyes flickering with tenderness and pride. "You did it all yourself, Goldilocks," he said gently. "And I don't know another woman in the world who would have covered the kind of territory we did today without so much as a whimper." He ruffled her sweat-darkened curls in a light caress. "You're quite a lady."

Kelly felt as glowingly proud as the day when she'd gotten her first lead story. She could feel the pleasure sing through her veins, and she experienced a sudden burst of energy.

"Then let me go with you," she urged impulsively. "We'll both rest when we've found that transport."

He shook his head again. "There's no reason for your going. Stay here and rest. We may be on the road all night. Carmen gave me a lead that looks fairly promising, so I should be back shortly."

Then, as Kelly still continued to look up at him with a stubborn frown on her face, Nick gave an exasperated groan and bent to give her a quick, hard kiss on her lips. "Look, Lois Lane, let Superman do his stuff. Okay? I swear that as soon as you get your second wind, I'll let you fight the very next dragon we run across."

Kelly smiled reluctantly. "You promise?" she asked lightly.

"I promise. The very next dragon that appears, I play maiden in distress to your Saint George." He outrageously fluttered his dark lashes.

Kelly giggled helplessly and threw up her hands. "Okay, you win," she said, crossing to a table and dropping down in a chair. She tossed her jacket on the chair next to her. "I'll wait here."

He rewarded her with such a warm smile that she felt breathless. "I think I'd better treasure this victory," he said wryly. "I have an idea I'm not going to have too many of them." He strolled over to the table and dropped his own jacket on it. "I almost forgot to give you this." He reached into the deep side pocket of the black jacket and pulled out a red bandanna-wrapped object and handed it to her casually.

"My Leica!" she exclaimed delightedly, when she had unfolded the bandanna from around the camera. "But how? I thought it was burned up in the balloon."

"Pedro's men managed to salvage some of our belongings from the wreckage. Pedro himself confiscated the camera. Unfortunately, our papers were burned to ashes."

"Then how did you get hold of it?" Kelly asked, running her hands over the camera. She'd thought that she would never see it again, and having it suddenly returned was like being given a wonderful gift.

"I played Pedro one last hand this morning while you were having breakfast," he replied, grinning. "I hope you really wanted that camera, sweetheart. When he lost, he offered to lend me one of his men's horses to ride to the village if I let him keep the camera. I thought you'd rather keep the Leica."

"Oh, yes," she said softly, her green eyes misting. "My father used this Leica for as long as I can remember. I haven't used any other camera since the day he died."

"Good." He turned and strolled toward the door. "Then I won't have to face that belligerent temper of yours for making you take a six-hour hike in the blazing sun." He waved casually, stepped through the door, and closed it softly behind him.

Kelly sat where he had left her, still holding her precious Leica and staring at the closed door, a bemused smile on her face. Nick, too, had made that miserable hike when he could have been riding in comparative comfort if he had been willing to let the bandit leader keep the camera. Her lips curved in a tender smile as she remembered just how hot and weary Nick had looked when they reached Matzalea. She felt a strange melting sensation somewhere near her heart.

Now after going through so much for her already, he was canvassing the village instead of resting. Kelly frowned and straightened slowly in her chair. Meanwhile, she was sitting here doing nothing, leaving it all to him. Well, she wasn't about to wait until a dragon appeared over the horizon for her to fight. She'd just go hunt one up on her own.

Kelly got briskly to her feet and marched toward the door beside the bar in search of her lethargic hostess.

It was almost six o'clock when O'Brien returned to the cantina, and Kelly was beginning to feel the faint stirrings of anxiety. Therefore, it was with profound relief that she saw him walk through the door and pause a moment to let his eyes adjust to the dimness after the glare of the street. It was only an instant before his gaze circled the room and spotted her sitting at a table in the corner of the cantina.

A flashing smile lit his dark face. He strolled slowly over to the table and dropped down into the chair across from her own. "Mexicali Rose, I assume," he said solemnly. "You've been busy, Goldilocks."

"I feel more like a Salvation Army reject." Kelly looked down at the flounced red cotton skirt that she was wearing with the low-necked white peasant blouse. They both belonged to Carmen Rodriguez, and Kelly's petite form was lost in them. The only way she had been able to get the skirt to stay up was to tie a black sash tightly around her slim waist. The peasant blouse was utterly impossible, hanging on her like a sack, and the low neckline persisted in slipping off her shoulders. "But I had to wear something while Carmen was washing my clothes."

"You've had a bath, too," he noticed, his eyes traveling over her clean, shining face and the sun-streaked ringlets that were still a trifle damp. "You look like a fresh-scrubbed baby."

"Carmen is heating water for your bath right now," Kelly said briskly. "She has some old clothing of her husband's that you can wear while she launders your own. The sun is so hot and the air so dry here, that the clothes should dry in a few hours."

"Oh, Lord, that sounds good!" Nick's gaze travelled over his dust-coated jeans and sweat-soaked shirt. "I bet I smell like a polecat."

"Well, now that you mention it," Kelly drawled and grinned impishly, "I was aware of a slight musky odor."

He chuckled. "Very delicately put, sweetheart. Am I allowed to ask how you managed to persuade our hostess to stir herself to such herculean efforts on our behalf?"

"Well, she wasn't about to exert herself for *me* without compensation," she replied. "I'm sure you would have had better luck with her. But she did take a fancy to my jade ring fortunately. It bought us baths, laundry services, and a meal. I must say it was a bit difficult communicating with her in sign language, however."

"You've supplied our every need, Kelly," Nick said slowly, reaching over to take her hand in his and looking down at her bare ring finger thoughtfully. "It was a very pretty ring. Did you place a high value on it, Goldilocks?"

She shrugged carelessly. "Of course not," she lied. "It was just an inexpensive dinner ring. I'll replace it when I get back to San Francisco. Did you find transport for us?"

He was still staring down at her hand, his thumb absently stroking her ring finger. "Yes, I think I found a way to get us out of here," he replied quietly. "But there's a small catch."

"There always is." Kelly sighed. "What is it this time? Another poker game with my fair body as the stakes?"

He shook his head, his expression oddly grave. "It's a little more complicated than that, I'm afraid," he said, still looking down at her hand. "It seems that Matzalea possesses its own resident priest, a Father Juan Miguel. He lives in Matzalea but travels around the area periodically to conduct mass in outlying villages. He has an ancient Buick station wagon that's his pride and joy."

"Will he let us borrow it?" Kelly asked, her eyes alight with eagerness.

He shook his head. "No, but he offered to drive us to Acapulco himself. I'll naturally send a donation to his parish when I get back to the States to pay him back for his time and expenses."

"Well, then what's the problem?" Kelly asked, puzzled. "Everything's working out splendidly."

"Except for one minor detail," Nick replied. "Father Miguel seems to be a kindly and devout man, but no one could call him a member of the modern enlightened clergy. He's as old-fashioned and outdated as this village. He doesn't approve of an unmarried man and woman traveling around Mexico together."

"What!" Kelly exclaimed, "But that's positively archaic. Didn't you explain what I was doing with you?"

"I thought it best not to," he said quietly. "Father Miguel obviously has rather rigid ideas regarding a woman's place in life. I told him instead that you were my *novia.*"

"And what is that?" Kelly asked warily, her eyes narrowing.

"My fiancée," he translated. "I thought it might pacify his moral code if we were at least engaged."

Her eyes widened. "And did it?" she asked carefully.

"No," he replied bluntly. "He wants to marry us at once before he'll agree to chauffeur us to Acapulco."

"Marry?" Kelly's mouth dropped open in shock, and she could feel her breath catch in her throat. "But that's impossible," she choked out. "Couldn't you talk him out of it?"

"Why do you think I was so long returning? Father Miguel is a very stubborn man, and he's holding all the aces. He has the only wheels in town."

"But surely there's something we can do," Kelly protested, nervously biting her lower lip. "We can't just give in to him on something as important as this. It's like something out of a Victorian melodrama."

"The only other option is a sixty-mile hike to the next village with no guarantee that we'd have better luck there," he said soberly. "As I said, the good father is holding all the aces."

"But . . ." Kelly trailed off helplessly, her jade eyes wide and troubled in her suddenly pale face.

Nick's hand tightened comfortingly on hers. "It's not the end of the world, you know. There's a distinct possibility that the marriage wouldn't even be legal in the States. Even if it is, there shouldn't be any trouble getting it annulled. It's not as if it's an irrevocable step, Kelly."

"No, I suppose not," she said dazedly. She was feeling a peculiar tightness in her throat, and she felt foolish tears brim in her eyes. What in the world was the matter with her that his casual dismissal of any permanent ties between them should cause this aching pain? "You think we should do it, then?"

"I don't think we have much choice," he said quietly, his eyes intent on her troubled face. "You agree?"

She drew a shaky breath and then tried to shrug carelessly. "Why not?" she asked flippantly, over the slight lump in her throat. "After all, you're risking much more than I am. You're the one who's rich as Croesus. How do you know that I won't hold you up for some exorbitant bundle in alimony?"

"I know," he said softly, his gaze holding her own.

"I know." It was an incredibly intimate moment the world narrowing to include just the two of them; they seemed bound in a golden, timeless haze.

Kelly was not aware how long she was held in that mesmerizing spell. She was vaguely aware of Carmen Rodriguez entering the cantina, undulating over to their table, and speaking to Nick. Kelly didn't even glance at Carmen until Nick reluctantly released her hand, turned to smile warmly at the cantina owner, and answered her with a brief, "*Gracias.*"

He turned back to Kelly. "It's my turn for a bath," he said. "Would you like to come and scrub my back?" His lips were curved in his usual mocking smile. It was as if that instant of sudden breathless rapport had never existed.

Kelly drew a deep breath and carefully composed her own expression. "I don't believe so," she replied lightly. "If you need any help, I'm sure that the merry widow will be more than happy to oblige." That fact was more than evident, she thought crossly, as she gazed with extreme displeasure at the plump, beaming cantina owner, who stood waiting for Nick to accompany her. She positively glowed with blatant invitation.

Nick rose to his feet and grinned down at her. "But I'm an engaged man now," he said, his eyes twinkling mischievously. "I'm quite sure that Father Miguel would never approve of such goings on."

Her lips curved in a reluctant smile. "And how long are you going to remain an engaged man?" she asked. "When does Father Miguel intend to tie the knot?"

"He suggested that we stroll over to the church about sundown," he answered casually. "I'll have a bath and make myself presentable, and we'll leave after our meal. Okay?"

"Okay," she said just as matter-of-factly. She made a face. "I suppose I'd better not change back into my own clothes as I'd planned. If the priest is as old-fashioned as you say, I doubt if he'd be pleased if I showed up for the nuptials in jeans."

"You're probably right," Nick replied, as he gestured politely for Carmen to precede him from the room. "Besides, I find that earthy peasant look very fetching." Without waiting for a reply, he followed their hostess to her rooms at the rear of the cantina.

Kelly didn't feel at all fetching some two hours later when they arrived at the chapel on the outskirts of the small village. She felt unattractive and terribly nervous and slightly sick to her stomach as they walked into the tiny vestibule.

O'Brien's keen glance raked her pale face and wide, frightened eyes in swift appraisal before his hand closed bracingly on her elbow. "If I wasn't so confident of my devastating charm, I might be offended by your unbridelike demeanor, Goldilocks. You look scared to death. I'm not really a bluebeard, you know."

"Sorry," she apologized, moistening her lips nervously. "It's just that I haven't done this before." She smiled tremulously. "I know little girls are supposed to have romantic fantasies about their wedding and marriage, but I never did. I just never thought about it. I guess I'm still suffering from shock." She had been carrying a mantilla, which she unfolded and put on.

"How flattering," Nick said dryly. "You may not be an eager bride, but you're certainly a lovely one in Carmen's mantilla."

Kelly touched the fragile lace. "It's perfectly beautiful, isn't it?" She looked up at him. "It was very generous of her to offer it, considering how disappointed she was when you told her we were going to be married. Tell me, did you soothe her feelings by letting her scrub your back, after all?"

"No, sweetheart, I scrubbed my own back," he said solemnly. "Though I did regard it as a monumental sacrifice."

"I don't know whether to believe you or not. She certainly managed to find you a more attractive wedding outfit than she did me."

Nick was wearing his own freshly laundered black jeans, but the white linen shirt with its exquisitely delicate flower design embroidered in fine white thread was truly beautiful. Carmen's husband must have been smaller than Nick, for it fit a bit tightly over his shoulders and hugged his lean waist. He had left a few buttons open at the throat for comfort, and his strong throat and muscular chest looked almost aggressively virile against the delicacy of the white embroidered linen.

"It's a little fussy for my taste, but I thought I'd try to do you proud," he said casually. "It's not every day that a man marries such a ravishing creature as Kelly McKenna."

"You *know* I look absolutely dreadful," Kelly wailed miserably. "Not only do these outsize clothes make me look like a rag bag, but my hair is a complete mess, and I don't even have any lipstick on." She glowered at him. "While you look perfectly gorgeous."

He grinned. "Men aren't gorgeous, Goldilocks," he corrected. "I'll grant you that I'm an exceptionally handsome devil, though."

"You're gorgeous," she repeated emphatically. "And it's just not fair."

He went suddenly still, the laughter fading from his face. "You really mean that," he said quietly. "I thought you were joking, but you really don't know how beautiful you are."

"Save the blarney, Nick. Even when I'm at my best, I know I'm not exceptional."

He gave her a curiously tender smile. "Aren't you?" he asked gently. He cupped her face in his two hands and looked down into her eyes. "There must be something radically wrong with my perception then. You appear most exceptional to me, love." He cocked his head thoughtfully. "Now, let's see where I miscalculated. Two very ordinary eyes that are sometimes the hue of grass after a spring shower and at other times as vibrant as emeralds." He brushed her lids with a kiss as light as butterfly wings. "Nothing unusual there." One lazy finger twisted a silky ringlet. "Hair that's touched with shining golden ribbons of color and curls around my finger as if it loves me. There's no real reason for me to find it appealing." His hand left her hair to touch the curve of her cheek. "As for the rest of your features, I'm sure there are thousands of women more beautiful, if you took time to look for them. Who wants strength and intelligence and a glowing *joie de vivre* when one can have cold, classical perfection?" He kissed her lightly on the lips as she gazed up at him in dazed bewilderment. "Yes, I'm sure you're right, sweetheart. There's nothing extraordinary about you."

Kelly was silent for an instant as she struggled to free herself from the velvet cloud of intimacy that he had created about her. "I'm glad you agree," she finally managed huskily. "You certainly know how to raise a girl's morale, Nick O'Brien."

"I didn't mention that curvy little body, which could bring a mummy back to life," he said softly. "That's certainly not exceptional either."

She laughed. "Okay! I surrender. I'm gorgeous, too!"

"Then shall we two gorgeous people go find Father Miguel and be joined in holy wedlock?" Nick asked. "I'm sure he's waiting anxiously to see if I'm going to make an honest woman of you."

She tucked her arm in his and said softly, "By all means, let's not disappoint the padre."

The first impression she had when she met Father Juan Miguel was that he looked more like Friar Tuck from Robin Hood's merry band than the old-fashioned, narrow-minded clergyman of O'Brien's description. In his early sixties, his short, rotund body and kind, laughing dark eyes were warmly appealing. He had only a sparse circle of gray hair bordering his head. His handshake was firm and hearty when O'Brien introduced them, and though the priest could speak no English, he managed somehow to convey both his pleasure and enthusiasm in performing their nuptials. With him was a middle-aged Mexican couple, who smiled and bobbed their heads in pleasure when the priest introduced them in Spanish. The witnesses, Kelly thought, as they walked to the altar.

Kelly felt strangely remote as she stood at the altar and let the incomprehensible Spanish words flow over her, responding dazedly when Nick urged her and otherwise mentally floating above the simple ritual. The whole scene was incredibly dreamlike, she thought: the austere interior of the chapel with its stark white walls and ancient pews; the golden rays of the setting sun pouring through the narrow windows and forming checked patterns of brilliant light and shadowy darkness on the ornate crimson and gold altar cloth; and the crucifix, beautifully wrought of ivory and bronze.

Nick's face was as bewilderingly bizarre as the rest of their surroundings. Perhaps it was that hazy golden twilight dimness that caused his expression to appear so set and stern as he answered the priest with ringing firmness. She was so absorbed in her fascinated appraisal of the lean, strong planes of O'Brien's face that it startled her when he turned and bent down to gently kiss her lips.

"Is it over?" she whispered, her jade eyes wide and childlike in her pale face. The delicate white lace mantilla floated over her shining curls with a graceful purity that reminded Nick more of a child at her first communion than of a bride.

He shook his head gravely, and his expression still had that puzzling element of sternness. "No," he said simply. "Most people consider this just the beginning."

Then, before Kelly could question this puzzling statement, Father Miguel was extending his hand in enthusiastic congratulations while he delivered a long discourse in Spanish that might have included advice, benediction, and general good wishes. She must ask Nick what he had said later, Kelly thought. The couple also smiled and spoke to them in Spanish. After signing papers, Kelly and Nick said goodbye to the couple and turned to Father Miguel, who gestured for them to follow him.

"Are we leaving now?" Kelly asked, startled. "I've got to go back to the cantina and change my clothes and return these to Carmen."

Nick had his arm firmly at her waist and was propelling her steadily after Father Miguel's plump, hurrying figure. "Don't worry about it," he said. "There'll be plenty of time to do that tomorrow morning."

"Tomorrow morning?" Kelly asked, bewildered. "But aren't we leaving for Acapulco this evening?"

Nick shook his head. "We'll leave Matzalea a little before noon tomorrow." His lips curved in a smile. "Do you think anyone with a code as rigid as Father Miguel's would sanction a newlywed couple starting out on their wedding night?"

"Then where are we going?" Kelly asked. They had left the chapel and were hurrying down the dusty main street of the village, trying to keep pace with the padre.

"Father Miguel said he had a wedding present for us," Nick answered.

"We can't take a present from him," Kelly protested. "He's been far too generous already."

"To refuse his gift would be an insult," Nick said. "We'll accept it graciously, and I'll arrange to send something of equal value as a thank-you present, once we get back to San Francisco."

"I guess that would be best," Kelly agreed a trifle

breathlessly, as she took a skip to keep up. "But where is he taking us?"

"I think we're there," Nick said, as Father Miguel paused at the stoop of a small, shabby adobe house. He fumbled in his habit, drew out an old-fashioned brass key, unlocked the door, and threw it open before turning to Nick and handing him the key. The priest had a beaming smile on his cherubic face. He proceeded to issue another long-winded discourse, and then he made the sign of the cross and turned and walked quickly away in the direction of the chapel.

More confused than ever, Kelly stared after him. She was barely aware of the gentle pressure of Nick's arm as he urged her into the adobe house and shut the door. It was almost completely dark outside now, and it was so dim inside the adobe hut that very little of the interior was discernible.

Nick left her side, strode a few feet away to what possibly could have been a table, and fumbled for a moment. Then there was a flare illuminating the darkness as he lit the white candle in its cheap black wrought-iron holder and replaced it on the table.

"What is this all about, Nick?" Kelly asked, frowning uncertainly. "Where are we?"

"We are now standing in the middle of Father Miguel's wedding present," Nick said wryly. "He arranged to have this house put at our disposal by one of his flock for our wedding night. Welcome to honeymoon hotel, Goldilocks!"

Six

"You've got to be kidding!" Kelly said in disbelief, shaking her head as if to clear it. Recalling the little ceremony at the door when Father Miguel handed Nick the key and blessed them, she had a sinking sensation that he wasn't. "Couldn't you talk him out of it?"

Nick shook his head. "We discussed that, remember? This wedding night is the padre's gift to us." He smiled. "I suppose I'd better scratch the idea of sending the padre a similar gift from San Francisco."

"Very funny," Kelly said caustically. "But that doesn't solve the problem of us having to spend the night in this blasted nuptial chamber. What are we going to do?"

Nick stretched, then strolled slowly over to where she stood by the door. His expression was tender as he gazed down at her troubled face. "I think you know the answer to that, Kelly," he said quietly.

"We're going to make full use of Father Miguel's little gift. I'm going to take you to bed and love you all through the night. If you'll be honest with yourself, you'll admit that it's what we both want."

She inhaled sharply and experienced an odd sensation of profound relief that was dizzyingly bewildering. Why should she feel relief when she'd been fighting this sensual takeover since she had first met Nick O'Brien?

She pulled her own gaze away from Nick's tenderly seductive one. "Physically, perhaps," she said nervously, moistening her lips. "But we both agree that we want nothing to do with an emotional commitment, and how can we keep the two from overlapping?"

Her eyes fastened on the pulse in his throat. "It would be crazy to begin an affair. It would be the ultimate no-win situation, and you warned me about that, remember?"

She could feel her own heart pounding as if it were trying to leap out of her body. He was not even touching her, but she could feel that honeycomb of breathless intimacy enfold them. Every nerve and muscle in her body was keyed up and waiting for him. She could hear her own voice arguing and protesting, but it was like those moments at the church when everything was curiously dreamlike. And all the time there was the waiting. Waiting for the words to be said. Waiting for the ritual of protest and rejection to be over. Waiting for the first chords of the music to start and the dance to begin.

"But then we've already established that you're addicted to that very thing," Nick said thickly. "And God knows I want you so much that I don't give a damn about possible fall-out from our coming together tonight. Look at me, sweetheart."

Her eyes lifted slowly to meet his, and she knew that the waiting was almost over. That odd feeling of inevitable "rightness" was with her again, and it brought with it a curious serenity. In the flickering candlelight, his face looked both powerful and sensual, but there was the same gravity and subtle tension in his expression that she had noticed at the church.

"I don't want to seduce you," he said hoarsely, the words coming out jerkily. "Though Lord knows I may give up and do it anyway if you don't give in soon. I want you to come to me as freely and joyously as I come to you. Let me pleasure you, love."

Those last, beautifully old-fashioned words had such a graceful Edwardian dignity, Kelly thought. She could feel the last vestige of resistance flow out of her.

She smiled tremulously. "I don't know much about this," she said faintly. "I've read all the books, of course, but you could probably have written one on the subject. I may disappoint you."

Nick exhaled almost explosively, his body's tenseness relaxing infinitesimally. "No chance of that. Judging by the few samples I've had, your potential is out of sight, Goldilocks." A warm smile illuminated his face. "Lord, I'm glad, Kelly!"

"So am I," she said simply. It was true. Now that the decision was made, the excitement and anticipation she was experiencing were mixed with a wild, singing happiness. There were no doubts and no regrets, only serene contentment. She wanted to give and receive all the gifts of physical pleasure that he had promised her. She wouldn't worry about the pain of possible parting tomorrow. Tonight she was going to let Nick lead her into the realm of passion that before him she had never even wanted to experience.

He reached out and pushed the white lace mantilla from her hair so that it fell about her shoulders. "I'm almost afraid to touch you," he said ruefully. "I want you so much that I'm tempted to reach out and grab, and you're a virgin, damn it!" He suddenly stepped back and drew a deep breath. "I've got to get out of here." He shifted her gently aside and opened the door.

"Where are you going?" Kelly cried, her eyes widening with shock and distress.

He looked over his shoulder, his expression grim. "We were married tonight. I may not know a hell of a lot about virgins, but I do know that brides are supposed to be allowed a time of preparation while the husband takes the traditional smoke. I intend to make sure that you get everything that you're entitled to." He smiled wryly. "It'll also give me a chance to cool off."

"But you don't smoke!" Kelly wailed. She was feeling nervous and shy enough already without Nick leaving her to her own devices. "I don't want you to go."

"So I'll take a walk," he said stubbornly. "We're going to do this right, Kelly. Fifteen minutes." The door closed behind him.

Kelly stared at the closed door in exasperation. Who would have dreamed that suave, sophisticated Nick O'Brien would pull something as Victorian as this, for heaven's sake? Now what was she supposed to do until he deigned to return after giving her "time"? She glanced restlessly about the room. It was really rather sweet. It evidently combined both dining and sleeping facilities. Besides the oak table there were four wooden chairs, the backs hand-carved decoratively in floral designs. Perhaps the owner of the cottage was a carpenter, she mused. The other finely carved furniture in the room seemed to bear out that premise. There was a chest by the white chenille-covered double bed that was really a work of art, and the bedposts were also carved with the same flowering petal and leaves design that was on the chairs. That carpenter had been really enamored of flowers, she thought. There was even a crudely painted picture of a lovely poinsetta painted on dried bark canvas on the wall over the bed.

She wandered over to take a better look at it. It was then that she noticed the white nightgown laying on the bed. She hadn't seen it before because it was the same white as the chenille spread. It had obviously been laid out for her use, and she felt her throat tighten a little at the thoughtfulness of the gesture. A white nightgown for the bride. What a touching thing to do. She wondered if the woman who had been their witness was also their generous hostess.

It took only a moment to slip out of Carmen's clothes and into the nightgown. The thin cotton gauze was simple, with a boat neck and no sleeves at all. It fell from her shoulders in a loose, graceful line to the floor. It was too large for her, but it didn't take away from the allure. The gauze was really shockingly thin. Kelly frowned uncertainly as she noticed that the pink of her nipples showed clearly through the material. She wondered how much more of her was revealed in that flickering candlelight. Well, she refused to worry about it. This was her wedding night, wasn't it? She carefully folded Carmen's clothes, then padded barefoot across the rough wooden floor to place them neatly on a chair by the table. She returned to sit on the side of the bed, her hands folded before her, to wait for Nick.

It would probably be at least another five minutes before he came back, she thought crossly. Who had ever conceived the idiotic idea that a bride needed time to steel herself for an experience that she was utterly wild for? She was surprised that Nick would pay any attention to such an outmoded custom; he was probably the most eccentric, unconventional man she had ever met, she thought. So why had he insisted on this very proper and conventional ritual? He had wanted her as much as she had wanted him in that moment when he had walked out the door.

The physical signs had been blatantly obvious, yet he had subdued them and walked away. Was it a sort of quixotic gift that he was giving her to show that he respected and cared about her feelings? There was no other explanation. A surge of happiness flooded through her at the realization. Oh, God, what a beautifully stupid thing to do! Would she ever know all the intricate facets behind that brilliant facade?

They had become so close in the last few days that she'd absorbed an incredible amount of information about his character without really thinking about it. His intelligence went without saying, but she had also found him courageous, patient, and incredibly tolerant. Though some of their experiences had been terrifying, she realized to her amazement that she had never once really regretted her decision to come with Nick. In fact, she knew now that when he was no longer with her, the days would prove to be dull and zestless.

Zestless? She shook her head, as the thoughts running through her head took on a frightening significance. She had always enjoyed life to the hilt, seeing each new day as an adventure. Now she was admitting to herself that because one Nick O'Brien might someday walk away, that he could turn that adventure into a desolate wasteland. How could the absence of one man make such a staggering difference?

"I couldn't wait any longer," Nick said huskily. She hadn't been aware of the door opening, but there he stood in the doorway. He was lithe and muscular, strong and virile. And the expression on his dark, lean face was beautifully taut and hungry. And then she knew the answer to all the questions that she had been asking herself.

She leaped to her feet and grabbed at the bedpost to steady herself, for she was suddenly dizzy with the knowledge that had burst on her like an exploding nova.

O'Brien closed the door behind him and then turned to look at her as she stood by the bed clutching the carved bedpost tightly, her whole body tense and poised as if to fly away. The flickering glow of the candle explicitly outlined her small figure in the sheer gauze gown. "Lord, you're beautiful!"

It was only after he had crossed the few yards separating them that he noticed the strange startled look in her wide green eyes. She was staring up at him as if he were a terrifying stranger.

A frown darkened his face. "What's wrong? God help you if you've changed your mind, Kelly. I've just about reached the end of my patience."

She shook her head, and her long lashes lowered to mask her eyes. She took one step forward and pressed herself to his lean, hard body, slipping her arms about his waist and nestling her head like a loving child against his chest. "No, I haven't changed my mind," she whispered, her words muffled.

"Then what's wrong?" he asked in exasperation. His arms went automatically around her and absently began rubbing her back through the thin cotton. "Why the hell were you looking at me like that?"

She wanted to answer, "Because I looked at you and suddenly realized that I love you. Because I'm scared to death thinking of life without you." Instead, she nestled deeper in his arms and said, "I guess you startled me when you came in. I wasn't expecting you yet. And this gown isn't exactly modest— perhaps I'm a little embarrassed."

"You have no need to be. You look like a very erotic Egyptian princess," he said thickly, his hands sliding down to cup her buttocks and press her up to his aroused loins. "*Very* erotic."

Kelly gasped as she felt his hardness through the thinness of the gown. It was as if she were naked, she thought. Then her lips curved wryly as she realized that this was almost the case. "For a man with total recall, that simile is pretty far off the mark," she said faintly, as his lips grazed her temple in a kiss as light as the brush of rose petals. "I don't think there are any blond Egyptians."

His lips moved down to nibble delightfully at her earlobe. "There are, you know," he said absently. "As a matter of fact, there's a band of Bedouins—"

He was abruptly silenced as she turned her head swiftly and closed his lips in a kiss of lingering sweetness. "Shut up," she whispered. "I don't give a damn about your blasted Bedouins."

He chuckled, his blue eyes twinkling. "You shouldn't be so narrow-minded, love," he said softly, as he nibbled at her lower lip. "There's something you can learn from every culture. Remind me to tell you about some of the Bedouin's unique sexual practices." His lips parted hers, and his tongue begun a hot, leisurely exploration that caused her body to arch against his and a low moan to start in her throat. His hands moved around to caress her breasts through the thin gauze, and the combination of his hard hands and the abrasiveness of the gauze aroused her even more. "On second thought, I'll demonstrate them," he said hoarsely, as his lips left hers. "But not until you graduate from the novice class, sweetheart."

He picked her up swiftly and laid her on the white chenille coverlet. He stood looking down at her, his face darkly intent as his hands unbuttoned his white linen shirt. His gaze traveled over her in frank enjoyment. "I love the way those perky pink nipples poke against that little bit of nothing as if they're trying to get out," he said teasingly. He shrugged off the shirt and threw it carelessly aside. "Let's help them, shall we?" He sat down on the bed beside her and leaned down to kiss each pink bud lingeringly and then proceeded to lick and bite at the taut tips through the transparent material until she was clutching at his dark head and making whimpering sounds deep in her throat. He raised his head to examine his work, his face flushed and sensual and his aquamarine eyes glazed. "Yes, I think it's definitely time we let them loose."

He sat her up gently, and it took only an instant to ease the gown up to her waist and pull it over her head. He tossed it on the floor with his shirt. Sitting on the side of the bed, he gazed at her for a long moment, his eyes committing every silky curve to memory.

Kelly felt as if she were going up in flames as he slowly bent and sucked gently at one breast while he kneaded the other with a brisk, forceful motion. The tactile contrast was terribly arousing, and she ran her hands lovingly over the wiry pelt of hair on his chest, then to the smoothness of the muscles of his shoulders. "You feel so alive," she whispered dreamily, closing her eyes to better enjoy the sensations that Nick's lips and her own hands were telegraphing to her. She felt almost weak with pleasure. "I never dreamed that anyone could feel so wonderful. Do all men feel this good?"

Nick's lips and hands suddenly left her breasts, and she opened her eyes in surprise. His forbidding expression made them open even wider. "Don't even think about trying to find out, Goldilocks," he said between clenched teeth. "Don't even think about it!"

"But I wasn't—" Kelly started hurriedly.

She didn't have time to finish before Nick's lips were crushing hers with a punishing ferocity, his hands tangling brutally in her curls to hold her head in place while he ravaged her mouth and tongue with almost savage passion. Then his hands ran probingly over her slim back down to her buttocks as if he wanted to brand each silky inch of her flesh with his stamp of possession.

She pressed closer to him even as his lips left hers and moved down to the crazily beating tom-tom in the hollow of her throat. "If you're wondering about your next man already, perhaps I'd better increase the tempo a bit to keep you interested," he said as his hands worked swiftly at his belt. Kelly could feel his heart thundering beneath her hands along with a new muscular tension bred by the anger that she could recognize in his voice. "I was trying to exert a little control considering your inexperience, but I wouldn't want to suffer later in comparison. So let's forget about patience and tenderness and move on to more exciting things."

He stood, turned his back to her, and stripped off the rest of his clothes. When he joined her this time on the bed, he pushed her into a reclining position on her back and lay down beside her, one hand casually cupping a breast while the other played idly with the curls at her neck. His lips moved in tiny, teasing kisses over her face and throat while his thumb teased her nipple. Kelly shivered as Nick threw one leg over hers and his lips moved to her ear, his tongue darting teasingly in and out.

"We've established how responsive your breasts are to loving," Nick said, supporting himself on one elbow as he looked down at her. His blue eyes were still stormy, and she knew that he had not recovered from that unreasonable flash of jealousy. "Let's see what else you like!"

And for the next ten minutes he did just that. His lips and tongue went over every inch of her body, caressing and teasing until she was ready to go mad with need. Then he started to use his teeth, gently biting and nibbling. She began writhing and arching her back. When he parted her limbs and started to bite gently on her inner thighs while his fingers began an even more intimate probing, she couldn't take it any more. She pulled his head up and looked into his eyes, her own brimming with tears.

"Nick, I'm going crazy," she whispered. "What are you trying to do to me?"

His expression was ruthlessly hard. He continued stroking her while he coolly appraised her wild, bright eyes and heaving breasts. "I want to make sure you remember me," he said tersely. His hand made a motion that caused her to arch in a fever of need, and she gave a little gasping moan. His lips curved in satisfaction. "And I think you will, won't you, sweetheart?"

How could she help it when he was making sure that her body was just one aching void waiting to be filled? she thought in exasperation. Was he so idiotically jealous that he was going to torment her like this indefinitely until he thought that she'd learned her lesson?

Evidently he felt she'd had enough, for he suddenly moved over her, parted her legs deftly, and slipped between them. His fingers were still involved in their erotic loveplay, and his eyes were narrowed on her face to catch every nuance of emotion he was evoking. "You'll remember me doing this to you, Kelly. Your body will remember and want me to do it again and again. Tell me how much you want me, Kelly. I want to hear you say the words."

He wanted to hear the words, did he? Well, she had had enough! "Yes, I'll remember this," she said hotly, her green eyes flaming up at him. "And you're so hellishly good at it that I'll probably want you to do it again." Her hands were knotted into small fists. "And, yes, I want you to give me what you've been teasing me with ever since I injured your ego with that perfectly innocent remark. I want you like crazy, you damn chauvinistic pig, but I sure as hell don't like you very much at the moment!"

His face was a mask of blank surprise as he looked down at her belligerent face, and then suddenly he began to laugh. His shoulders shook with the force of the mirth that continued to pour from him while Kelly looked up at him in angry puzzlement.

When he finally managed to subdue his laughter

to an occasional chuckle, he kissed her gently on the lips. "It's said that everyone in the world has a double, but don't let anyone tell you that's true, love. There's not another Kelly McKenna in the entire universe." His dark face was alight with laughter, and his eyes were blazing jewel-bright with tenderness and humor. "Will you let this poor egotistical chauvinist come into your sweet warmth and love you, Goldilocks?"

"Oh, yes," she said softly, beaming up at him in loving satisfaction. "By all means, yes!"

He was infinitely gentle at first, but that didn't last long. They had both been stretched to the limits of their patience by his lingering foreplay. His lips and hands ran feverishly over her in a hot ritual of passion as his hips moved with a strength and urgency that caused her to whimper and cry out his name in an agony of anticipation.

"That's right, call my name, love," he said, his breath rasping in his chest, his eyes on her face. "I love to hear you cry it out in that sexy little voice."

He got his wish only an instant later when she almost moaned it in an agony of ecstasy as the tension that had been mounting in quantum leaps suddenly exploded into a delirium of mind-shattering delight.

She didn't know how long it was before she was able to stop the trembling that was shaking her limbs and steady her breathing. They were lying side by side, and she had her head pressed into the hollow of Nick's shoulder. His arms still held her tightly. His heartbeat reverberating beneath her ear was just as fast as her own, she realized with satisfaction.

"Are you all right, love?" Nick asked gently, his lips brushing across her temple in a warm caress. "I didn't hurt you?"

"I don't know whether you did or not." Kelly sighed contentedly as she snuggled closer. "At that point

I couldn't have cared less. Lord, I don't know how anyone survives this sort of thing if it happens as often as I understand. It nearly blew me into smithereens!"

Nick chuckled in amusement. "Very delicately put, Goldilocks." His lips moved to the curve of her cheek. "It's the nature of the species to survive this particular experience, though I admit that all of them aren't this mindblowing. You're a very special lady, Kelly."

"I was okay, then?" she asked, tilting her head to look up at him earnestly. "I was a little nervous about that."

He kissed her lightly on the nose. "Oh, yes, you were definitely 'okay,'" he said softly. "We're as fantastic together as I thought we would be. God, you fit me like a glove, sweetheart. It was like coming home." He covered her breast gently with his hand. "I've only just left you, Goldilocks, and I'm already lonely for you."

Kelly felt a surge of heat running through her and that incredibly melting ache beginning again in her loins. Her eyes widened in surprise. "I think I want you again, too. How could it happen again so soon?"

Nick's blue eyes were warm with tenderness. "It seems we're better matched than I thought," he said, grinning mischievously. "I think you're going to prove a deliciously lusty wench." He gave her a quick, hard kiss, then pushed her firmly away. "Much as I'd love to oblige you, you're going to have to restrain yourself from attacking me for a bit, love." He stripped back the white chenille bedspread and then tucked both of them beneath the covers, settling her head once again in the curve of his shoulder.

Kelly's hand moved lazily to his chest and began to toy idly with the springy dark hair on his chest. "Why do we have to wait?" she asked curiously. "If we're both agreeable, it doesn't seem very reasonable."

"My enchantingly lovely Kelly, you were a virgin, for God's sake," he said patiently. "It's very reasonable indeed to let you rest and recover before I ravage that gorgeous little body a second time."

Oh, Lord, Nick wasn't going to be gallant again, was he? Was this another dratted Victorian misconception that Nick had unearthed about virgins?

"I don't need to recover," she said crossly. Nick's smooth, hard muscles under her hand were so beautifully powerful, she thought. "For Pete's sake, you didn't rape me, you made love to me. In case you didn't notice, I was quite willing."

"I noticed," he said. "Nevertheless, we'll wait awhile."

Oh, would they? Nick was assuming control again with that same infuriating arrogance. She might be a novice, but there was no way she would let Nick think he could have it all his own way.

"I'm sure you're right," she cooed meekly, her hands tracing patterns on his chest. "How lucky I am that you're willing to give poor little me the benefit of your vast experience, Nick." Her exploring fingers found a hard male nipple and teased it delicately. She could feel his chest contract as he inhaled sharply, and she almost purred with satisfaction. "Of course I'll abide by your decision," she went on docilely. "But I'm sure you won't mind if I amuse myself while we're waiting for me to recover."

"Kelly!" Nick said warningly, then gave a convulsive shudder as her hands moved down and a tantalizing pink tongue stroked teasingly at the nipple while her small hands moved curiously over his hard stomach. "Kelly, stop that, damn it!"

"But why, Nick?" she asked innocently, as her hand traveled leisurely down the hard column of his thigh. "Isn't that what you did to me? I'm only following your example." His thigh felt so different from her own. It was rough to the touch with its dusting of hair and the firm muscles that were tensing at her teasing exploration. She moved closer so that her breasts brushed enticingly against him.

"I'm just curious. You can understand that, Nick, you have such an inquiring mind yourself. But I don't want to bother you when you're so determined to hold to your good intentions. You just lie there, and I'll simply experiment a little on my own."

"Kelly, you little devil, you're driving me crazy, and you know it," Nick gasped in a strangled voice. "I'm going to get you for this."

"That's what I'm earnestly working toward," she said demurely, her hands moving slowly to the inside of his thigh. "Now, let's see, what do I do next?"

"You get laid, damn it." He suddenly rolled her over on her back and looked down at her with a curious mixture of exasperation and tenderness. She noticed with satisfaction that his eyes were blazing with desire and his chest was heaving with the force of his breathing. "You win, you bold hussy. You don't know what's good for you, and you've made quite sure that I don't care at the moment."

She looked up into his beautifully sensual face, her gaze lovingly tracing the powerfully molded planes of his cheekbones. "I know what's good for me," she said, pulling him slowly down to her. "I know."

When Kelly woke the next morning, she was still curled in Nick's arms, her head on his chest and her arms holding him in possessive delight. How lovely it would be to wake every morning with the throb of Nick's heartbeat in her ear and the warm security that those strong arms gave her, she thought dreamily. Still half asleep, she started to brush little affectionate kisses on his chest. She was interrupted most rudely when Nick's hand came down on her derriere with a distinctly ungentle slap.

"Stop that, Goldilocks," he said lightly, his voice depressingly wide awake. "You know damn well where that leads, and we haven't got time." He chuckled. "I was just lying here watching you sleep and thinking how you looked like an innocent, sweet baby. Then the first thing you do even before you open your eyes is try to seduce me."

"I wasn't trying to seduce you," she protested. "I was merely being affectionate." She snuggled closer to him, and for a moment his arms tightened around her in a quick hug. Then, disappointingly, she felt his arms withdraw and the mattress shift as he rolled away from her and got out of the bed.

For a moment she didn't move but lay there with her eyes closed, unwilling to give up that lovely, drowsy euphoria. Then as she heard Nick moving briskly around, she reluctantly opened her eyes. He had pulled on his black jeans and was fastening his belt, and she watched him for a moment, admiring how downright sexy he looked. The dark denim material hugged his powerful thighs and buttocks lovingly, and without a shirt, his slim waist, flat belly, and powerful shoulders looked overwhelmingly virile.

"Where are you going?" she asked sleepily, rising up on one elbow to look at him.

He looked at her and grinned. "It's time we got on the road, wife. By the angle of that sun coming through the window, it must be almost noon, and Father Miguel said he'd meet us at the chapel at twelve-thirty." He reached for his white shirt, slipped it on, and started to button it. "I'm going over to the cantina and see if I can persuade Carmen to heat us some water for baths."

Kelly sat up slowly and brushed her tousled curls away from her face. "I don't think you'll have any trouble there. Should I wait here a discreet length of time to give you an opportunity to 'persuade' her?"

Nick cocked an eyebrow. "That's definitely feline, Goldilocks," he drawled. He sat down on the bed beside her and proceeded to put on his socks and desert boots. "And completely unrealistic. I'd have to be a Superman, indeed, to be interested in another woman after the workout you gave me last night." He grinned teasingly. "I'm just a poor shell of the man that I was before one Kelly McKenna."

She hit him lightly on the arm with her fist. "Beast." She shook her head in wonderment at his bounding vitality when she was feeling so weary and languid. "You appear to be in very fine fettle to me."

"I put up a good front," he said lightly, then turned to face her, having finished putting on his desert boots. His eyes widened as he noticed how she had carelessly let the sheet fall to her waist, baring her creamy breasts. "But not nearly as good as you," he added huskily, his gaze flickering with the beginning of desire.

Kelly could feel the familiar heat begin to surge through her. "I'm glad you think so," she said breathlessly, not bothering to pull up the sheet.

It would be like locking the barn door after the horses had fled to display any hint of modesty now. Nick had enthusiastically explored every inch of her body the night before, in those long, heated hours of lovemaking. Their desire for each other had been just as insatiable the last time they had come together as the first time. No, more so, for they knew that each time had been more wildly exciting than the last as they had learned how to please each other. She would have thought that after last night she would have been sated, but she found now that Nick had only to look at her with that kindling passion in the depths of his eyes, and she was as eager as if he'd never touched her. And that look was definitely in his eyes right now, she thought happily.

Then to her dismayed chagrin, he reached out and pulled the sheet over her breasts and carefully tucked it under her armpits. "Stop tempting me, Kelly. I'm finding it difficult enough to keep my hands off you without your throwing that brand of invitation at me. This is our only chance to get to Acapulco, and we're not going to miss it just because I want to throw you in the sack and stay there for a week or so."

Kelly felt hurt. How could Nick so coolly control that fever in the blood that she found irresistible? she wondered. At the moment she didn't give a damn about Acapulco, or her story, or anything but him. Naturally, she couldn't expect him to feel the same way, she told herself gloomily. She was the one who was crazily in love. He probably looked on last night as just another enjoyable toss in the hay with an attractive, available female.

She looked away from him, her lashes masking the raw hurt that the thought brought. "Then you'd better hurry," she said, her voice a little throaty. "I'll join you at the cantina as soon as I've finished dressing."

Nick swore under his breath, and his hands were suddenly on her shoulders. "Now what the hell's the matter?" he asked, giving her a gentle shake. "You act like you've just been cruelly rejected when you know damn well that I'd like nothing better than to crawl back in bed with you. Don't you want to go to Acapulco?"

"Yes, of course," Kelly said firmly, smiling with forced brightness. "I have a terrific story to write, haven't I? Even better than the one I would have had if the balloon had actually reached Acapulco." She was staring determinedly at a delicately embroidered flower on the front of his shirt. "I think I may leave a few minor details out, however. I wouldn't want to make any of your harem jealous."

"Kelly, look at me, damn it," he ordered roughly. "You're building walls between us again, and there's no way I'm going to go back to square one after last night. Why the devil won't you tell me what's bothering you?"

"Because there's nothing wrong with me," Kelly said clearly. With no little effort she raised her eyes to meet his. "Perhaps I was a little disappointed that you didn't find me totally irresistible," she said flippantly. "But then I guess I couldn't really expect that with a man who has a little black book the size of the Manhattan white pages."

He gazed at her flushed, defiant face for a long moment, his own expression growing stormier by the second. "You have got to be the most exasperating woman I have ever had the misfortune to meet," he said, his hands tightening angrily on her bare shoulders. "I haven't got time now to probe beneath that barbed little shell you're hiding behind, but I'm not about to let you stay there for long, Kelly. We'll settle this when we get to Acapulco." He slowly released her and stood up, his eyes on her face. Then he whirled and strode angrily toward the door. "Be at the cantina in ten minutes, or I'll be coming back for you." He slammed the door violently behind him.

Kelly stared unhappily at the door for a moment before she slowly got out of bed and started to dress. She had said all the wrong things in all the wrong ways, she thought miserably. She couldn't have admitted to Nick how terrified she had suddenly become at the thought of returning to civilization, but she hadn't had to act like a jealous bitch. She shook her head as she thought of how angry Nick had been when he left. If she didn't gain control of her emotions and overcome her jealousy, she'd certainly drive Nick away from her. Yet how did she know that Nick wouldn't regard their arrival in Acapulco as the end of their romantic interlude, anyway?

Kelly inhaled sharply as that thought stabbed painfully through her. She didn't think she could bear it if Nick cut short their affair so abruptly. She must have time to prepare herself before they parted, or the parting would rip her to pieces.

She finished dressing, then swiftly made the bed and straightened the little room that now seemed very dear and familiar. She opened the door and gave the room one last nostalgic look before she closed it behind her and hurried down the dusty street toward the cantina.

Seven

The Acapulco Star Hotel was a fabulously beautiful modern structure located high on the cliffs overlooking the stunning blue waters of Acapulco bay. Stunning was definitely the descriptive word for any number of the aspects of this gorgeous resort town, Kelly mused, as Father Miguel's ancient gray Buick chugged steadily up the twisting road that led to the towering mammoth skyscraper at the top of the cliffs. The radiant, jewel-bright colors and sheer beauty of the town were almost an assault on the senses.

"Like it?" Nick asked quietly, his gaze on her face as she peered eagerly through the window of the passenger seat of the car. Nick was sitting between her and Father Miguel, and his hard, muscular thigh was lodged intimately against her own as he leaned over to point out various points of interest.

Kelly nodded. "Who could help it? I thought the Italian Riviera was spectacular, but this is absolutely incredible. I gather you've been here before?"

At his nod of assent she enthused, "I don't see how you could ever leave it!"

"Yes, you can," he said. "Think about it, sweetheart. I'd say you'd be able to take this leisurely jet-set atmosphere for a maximum of three weeks tops, before you went completely bananas. It's too easy for people like us. You don't even have to make the effort to go look for a magnificent view because there's one wherever you turn. There's no challenge if it's all laid out for you."

"Well, I fully intend to enjoy myself thoroughly while I'm here, despite your arrogant cynicism, Nick O'Brien," Kelly said loftily. "And if Acapulco is so boring, why did you decide to come back?"

"I didn't say it was boring, I merely said it wasn't my cup of tea," he said quietly. "I come here occasionally to relax and do some deep-sea fishing." His arm was on the back of the seat behind her, and he began to play casually with the curls at her nape. "You'll probably enjoy your stay here very much after the strain of the last few days. In fact, I'm looking forward to showing you the sights."

Kelly smothered a little sigh of relief. If Nick was making plans that included both of them, then he couldn't be thinking of suggesting that they go their separate ways just yet. On the trip from Matzalea, she had tried to repair the damage she had done and get back on at least companionable terms with Nick. This hadn't proved the easiest thing in the world with the verbose Father Miguel as chaperone. The priest had chattered away jovially in Spanish from the moment they had left the village the previous afternoon. She had thought that she would have an opportunity to smooth things over when they stopped for the night, but the humble hacienda where Father Miguel had chosen to break their trip had afforded no privacy whatsoever. Kelly had found herself sharing a bed with the lady of the house and her youngest child, while Nick and Father Miguel had bedded down on a mattress on the floor in the other room.

"That will be terrific," she said enthusiastically, her eyes on the glittering smoked glass and white stone of the hotel. "The Star is really lovely, but there's nothing very Latin about it, is there? Why did you choose this for your stay?"

"For the most pragmatic of reasons, I'm afraid. O'Brien Computers owns a large percentage of the Star, and the manager knows me. Since we have neither cash nor credit cards and absolutely no papers or identification, we're going to need all the help we can get to straighten out the mess we're in."

The mess, being marriage to one Kelly McKenna, she thought despondently. Well, she had known Nick felt that way. She must guard against having it hurt her so deeply when he put it into words. "How long do you think it will take?" she asked quietly, her eyes fixed on the red and white canopy at the front entrance of the hotel.

She could feel Nick's shoulders move against her own as he shrugged. "Who knows?" he said tersely. "I'll put a lawyer on it as soon as we get settled in at the hotel, but the fact that we have no papers isn't going to help things. We'll just have to be patient and wait it out. Our first priority will be to pull enough strings with the embassy to get us back in the States without proof of citizenship. It may be a very friendly border, but immigration has tightened up considerably since the wetback situation has received so much publicity lately. I'm afraid if you have a deadline for your story, you're going to have to call it in by phone. It will probably take at least a couple of weeks to cut through the red tape and get us out of here."

Kelly didn't dare look at him for fear that he would see the happiness radiating from her face. "I don't have a deadline," she said lightly. "I don't think Mac really even expected me to get the story. He was positively jubilant when I called him the evening we left and told him that you'd agreed to take me with you." Suddenly her eyes widened as a thought occurred to her, and she swiveled to face him. "Good heavens, you don't suppose they've called out the marines or anything because we're a little late in arriving?"

Nick shook his head. "Not yet," he said dryly. "A hot air balloon can't be called reliable transportation by the wildest stretch of the imagination. I'm sure they'll have assumed that we've just been delayed by adverse weather." Then he raised a dark brow inquiringly. "Unless you think your editor may have become alarmed that he hasn't heard from you?" There was a trace of hardness in O'Brien's tone that Kelly failed to detect as she considered the possibility.

Mac Devlin had been a good friend of her father's, and he still sometimes regarded her with maddening paternalism despite the tough, hard-boiled facade he presented. "I'd better call him as soon as possible," Kelly said, frowning. "Mac will probably be foaming at the mouth by this time. He gets uptight if I don't check in when I say I will."

"Then by all means we must let Mr. Devlin know at once," Nick said sarcastically. "We wouldn't want him to become upset, would we?" His face was granite hard as he continued harshly. "You never did tell me what your wager with Devlin entailed. Considering the fact of your inexperience, I doubt that the stakes were quite what I thought, but I'd be interested to know just what your editor would have received if you'd lost that bet."

She had no opportunity to reply, for Father Miguel pulled to a stop before the front entrance, and the passenger door was opened by a smiling, white-jacketed young Mexican. Kelly was helped from the car with a courtesy that spoke well for the service standards of the hotel. By the warmth of their greeting, it might have been a shiny new Rolls Royce that they'd arrived in rather than Father Miguel's rackety 1952 Buick.

She was about to follow the boy into the hotel when Nick put a detaining hand on her arm to stop her. "You'd better say your goodbyes to Father Miguel now," he said, turning her toward the priest, who had gotten out of the car and was standing beside it. "He's returning to Matzalea tonight, and he wants to visit a friend this afternoon before he sets out."

"But I thought surely he'd stay the night and have dinner with us," Kelly protested, as the priest turned his merry eyes on her disappointed face. Language barrier or not, she had grown to like the plump little priest very much on the long, uncomfortable journey. "Can't you persuade him to stay?"

Nick shook his head. "He has a baptism to perform day after tomorrow, and he says he must get back."

Kelly's hand was enfolded in the priest's warm clasp, and he began one of those long, rambling speeches that he seemed to favor. Darn it, the first thing she was going to do when she got back to San Francisco was to enroll at Berlitz for a crash course in Spanish. She couldn't even tell this warm, friendly man how much she appreciated his help. However, he seemed to be more than satisfied with the profound sincerity of her, *"muchas gracias."* He patted her cheek kindly and kissed her forehead. Then he shook Nick's hand, spoke rapidly to him, and got back into the car. Kelly felt Nick's arm slide casually around her waist while they stood watching Father Miguel turn the ancient car and with a final wave of his hand start down the hill.

"He seems like such a nice little man," Kelly said wistfully. "I wish I could have understood what he was saying to me."

Nick turned and propelled her toward the glass door being held open for them by the Mexican boy.

"That's very generous of you, considering the problems his actions have caused you," he said expressionlessly. "Let's hope you still feel as kindly toward him by the time we finish with the lawyers." They had arrived at the reception desk, and she had no opportunity to answer, for Nick was demanding to speak to John Sykes, the manager.

Twenty minutes later she was gazing admiringly around the strikingly luxurious lounge of the penthouse suite to which she'd been shown by a porter. It had taken O'Brien only a short time to be admitted to the hotel manager's office and to arrange for accommodations. He'd told her to go on up to the suite while he and Sykes contacted the embassy and saw what could be done about a reentry permit.

The accommodations that they'd been given were quite spectacular, and she wondered just how big a percentage O'Brien Computers owned to rate quarters like these. The lounge was carpeted in a lush hunter green that contrasted beautifully with the long white velvet couches and occasional chairs. There was a bar at one end of the room with a beautifully carved Aztec calendar on its rich mahogany surface. The sliding glass doors that led to the flower-bordered balcony were also hung with white velvet. There were three bedrooms opening off the lounge with adjoining baths, and the suite even contained a tiny, well-equipped kitchen.

At least she blended well with the color scheme despite the dusty, rumpled condition of her olive jeans and shirt, she thought wryly. This elegant apartment had probably never been graced with such a scruffily garbed resident before. Well, she couldn't do anything about her clothes, but she could at least get rid of some of the dust that had accumulated on her person.

She made a quick tour of the available bedrooms before reluctantly deciding against occupying the largest and most luxurious of the three. It was obviously the master bedroom, for it contained a huge king-sized bed and a bathroom that was almost sinfully luxurious. Since Nick had seen fit to quarter them in a suite with three bedrooms, perhaps he had no intention of their occupying the same bed now that they had returned to civilization. She would not court rejection by taking anything for granted.

No, she would take the pretty little guest room two doors down. A few minutes later she was reclining lazily in a white marble tub while the jetting spray of hot water turned the bubble bath that she'd sprinkled generously into the water into lovely pink bubbles. She lifted a large irridescent bubble carefully on one finger and admired its delicate beauty idly. There was something deliciously feminine about pink bubbles, she thought contentedly, and after days spent in jeans and a rather mannishly tailored shirt, she was ready to indulge in a little feminine pampering.

After turning off the water, she leaned back against the back of the tub, resting her head on the bath pillow and letting the tension and weariness gradually flow out of her. It was so wonderfully relaxing just to let everything go and not think about anything, that she felt almost drugged with pleasure. She would close her eyes just for a moment, she thought.

The gentle manipulation of the soft sponge against her shoulders was beautifully soothing, and she could have purred with contentment. Perhaps she did, for she heard Nick chuckle with amusement. Nick? She opened her eyes drowsily and met Nick's mischievous gaze. Somehow it seemed surprisingly natural to see him on his knees by the tub, the sleeves of his black shirt rolled up past the elbow, while he wielded the sponge with gentle strokes.

For a moment she stared at him sleepily, enjoying the treasured feeling that this intimate service gave her. Then she protested faintly, her jade green eyes bemused. "You shouldn't be here, Nick."

"Shhh, little love," he said almost caressingly. "You're tired. Let me take care of you, Kelly." The sponge brushed her throat gently. "Just relax and let me do it all."

Well, why not? She couldn't deny that she was enjoying his ministrations, and she was so lethargic that moving even one finger seemed to require a herculean effort. Nick's movements were curiously sexless as he carefully washed her from her shoulders to the sole of each small foot and then had her sit up away from the tub so that he could attend to her back. The sponge moved lazily up and down her spine while she sat dreamily enjoying the attention like a small child at her evening bath.

She felt a light kiss brush against her left shoulder blade and then the sponge was thrown into the water in front of her. "All right, sweetheart, that's almost all my willpower can withstand at the moment. It's time we got you out of here before I decide to join you."

He stood up and reached for a huge pink velour bath towel on the warmed rack above the tub. "Come on, angel, upsy-daisy!"

Kelly obediently stood up, and he wrapped her in the soft, fleecy towel before lifting her out of the white marble tub. He proceeded to pat her dry through the folds of velour. She stood quite still as he leaned forward to kiss her tenderly on the lips. "I could become addicted to this, you know," he said huskily.

"Me, too," she replied softly, her gaze fixed lovingly on his face. She wondered why she had felt not even a trace of embarrassment as he bathed her. She felt so close to him that it was as if he were an extension of her own body. She had heard that couples who had been married for decades sometimes had that rapport, but she had never expected to experience it herself.

"Come on, love," Nick said. "I've ordered us some lunch, and it should be arriving any minute." He kissed her again, this time on the tip of her nose, and drew her swiftly from the bathroom.

"I'm not exactly dressed to receive room service," Kelly said ruefully, looking down at her towel-draped figure. "And I absolutely refuse to put those jeans back on until they're laundered."

"No problem." Nick walked over to a built-in closet and opened the sliding doors. "The Star follows the custom of some of the better European hotels." He reached on the overhead shelf above the rack and pulled down a freshly laundered white terry robe. He grinned as he tossed it to her. "It's a shame to replace that fetching pink towel with anything so plebian. The only reason that I'm doing it is that I'm too damn jealous to let the waiter enjoy the same privileges that I'm accorded. Now while you slip that on, I think I'll take a quick shower. Let the waiter in when he rings, will you?" He strode swiftly toward the door of the bedroom and turned before going through it to say coolly, "I'm sorry if you have a particular fondness for this room, Kelly, but you'll have to move. We'll find the king-sized bed in the master bedroom much more comfortable." Without waiting for her reply, he was gone and didn't notice the expression of happiness on her face.

When he joined her for lunch in the living room twenty minutes later, he, too, was dressed in a calf-length white terry cloth robe, and his raven hair was damp and glossy from the shower.

Kelly looked down at her own white-robed figure and grimaced. "We look like Barbie and Ken dolls," she said. "Though, at the moment, I couldn't care

less as long as I can dig into that scrumptious meal."
She nodded to the white damask-draped table that
the waiter had wheeled before the glass terrace doors.
"Vegetable soup, salad, and red snapper." She sighed
blissfully as Nick politely seated her and went around
to his own chair. "Not even a hint of beans."

"I imagined that you'd had enough of the local
cuisine." Nick grinned as he shook out his napkin
and placed it on his lap. "They appear to have an
extremely talented chef judging by the raves from
the clientele. We just might be able to get through
our entire stay with nary a bean."

"Super," she said, closing her eyes ecstatically after the first delicious spoonful of the soup. Then her
eyes flicked open, and she started to eat in earnest.
"And how long is that stay likely to be?" she asked
casually. "Did you get in touch with the embassy?"

He nodded, a frown creasing his forehead. "There
may be a few problems that we hadn't counted on,"
he said slowly. "For one thing, until we substantiate
whether the marriage is actually legal, any immigration documents that they might arrange to have
issued would quite possibly be incorrect." He shrugged.
"They prefer that we let the lawyers sort out the
legalities before they get to work on our papers. It
shouldn't take more than a week or two."

"Well, I guess there's nothing we can do but go
along with what they suggest," Kelly said lightly,
trying not to show that she was happy at the delay.
"I found out a long time ago that you can't argue
with bureaucracy. A few weeks in Acapulco might be
quite bearable when you think about it." She grinned.
"Providing that I don't have to spend them in olive
green jeans and shirt. Any chance of you using
your clout with the manager to get a few charge
accounts approved for me? I noticed some really
smart boutiques in the lobby."

"I'm one step ahead of you, Goldilocks. Sykes has
already called and told the managers that you're to

have anything you want. The tab is to be put on my bill." He raised his hand as she started to protest. "It's all quite proper. We're married, remember?" His lips curved impishly. "You may even be tax deductible."

"Well, in that case I won't argue with you about it"—she hesitated—"until we get back to San Francisco."

He chuckled and shook his head. "I'm sure you will, sweetheart. I also told Sykes to have the boutiques send up a few basic essentials until you had an opportunity to make your own selections. They should be delivered later this afternoon."

"How very efficient of you," she said. "You fulfill my every need."

He looked up from his fish, and there was a devilish twinkle in his eyes. "I certainly intend to," he said softly. "That's why I told them to deliver your clothes 'later' this afternoon."

Kelly's eyes widened, and she could feel the color surge to her cheeks. Drat it, evidently she was not destined to get rid of that annoying habit of blushing. "I see," she said, lowering her eyes to her plate again quickly. "This fish really is excellent, isn't it?" she asked hurriedly.

She could feel Nick's amused gaze on her face. "Yes, excellent," he agreed solemnly. Then taking pity on her, he went on briskly. "After lunch you can use the phone in the master bedroom to make your phone calls. There's a separate line that I can use in here." He nodded at an elegant cream-colored push-button phone on the walnut end table by the couch. "I suppose I'd better call the home office and let my father know that I'm still alive."

"Your father is still president as well as chairman of the board of O'Brien Computers, isn't he?" Kelly asked. "I would think that he'd get a little upset with one of his chief executives taking the kind of chances you do, not to mention the filial emotions involved. Are you and your father very close?"

He shrugged. "Not very. I always made him feel a little uncomfortable, I think. He would have been much happier with a normal run-of-the-mill son. I can't say that he didn't do his best for me, though. He took all the psychological advice on the care and feeding of gifted children." His aquamarine eyes revealed a curious loneliness. "It wasn't his fault that he found it difficult to accept what I was."

"I'm sure you're wrong about him," Kelly said gently, her throat suddenly tight. "No father could help but be proud of such a son."

He shook his head, his expression bleak. "No, I'm not mistaken," he said tersely. "Don't waste your sympathy on me, Goldilocks. My father and I came to an understanding a long time ago. I conduct my independent research and stay out of my father's corporate and social paths. In return for that courtesy, he gives me license to take off whenever I get bored on whatever scheme takes my fancy."

"Such as taking a hot air balloon to Acapulco to try out a completely untested fuel formula," Kelly said, smiling at him in perfect understanding.

He grinned back at her and nodded. "Well, you've got to admit it wasn't boring."

"Yes, I have to admit that. We must thank your friend, the fuel inventor, for an exceptionally interesting balloon trip."

"Which reminds me, one of my phone calls must be to him to tell him that he's going to have to go back to the drawing board with that formula." Nick picked up the silver coffee pot from the table and filled Kelly's cup and then his own. His smile faded abruptly as he said, "I suppose you're very eager to contact Devlin. Are you going to tell me now what the terms of your wager were? You've been more than a little evasive on the subject."

"It would serve you right if I left you to wonder,"

she replied, making a face at him. "What a suspicious mind you have, Nick. Mac Devlin is old enough to be my father and very happily married as well." She took a sip of her coffee, appreciating the delicious flavor after the thick, syrupy brew that they'd been drinking on their journey. "But I don't mind satisfying your curiosity." She leaned lazily back in her chair and said cheerfully, "When I got back from the Middle East almost seven weeks ago, I had to spend a few weeks in the hospital with a case of malaria. Mac's something of a worrywart, and he refused to approve any overseas assignments for the next six months." She grinned impishly. "I'm afraid that I was making his life hell on earth with my nagging, so he proceeded to look around for something to get me off his back." She paused. "Enter one Nick O'Brien."

Her smile faded, and her eyes widened in alarm as she saw that Nick was definitely not amused. In fact, he was perfectly furious, his expression stormy and his blue eyes narrowed to slits.

"Do you mean to tell me that you just got out of the hospital a few weeks ago?" he asked.

"Why—yes," she faltered uncertainly. "But I'm perfectly well now. I told you that Mac's a bit overprotective."

"We've spent practically every moment together for the past five days," he said, emphasizing each word. "And you didn't see fit to tell me that even your editor considers your health below par?"

Why was he so angry? she wondered in exasperation. "Why should I reveal my entire medical history when it wasn't relevant? For God's sake, Nick, it wasn't important!"

"Not important? I could break your neck, Kelly McKenna!" His blue eyes were glaring into hers. "I let you walk *fifteen miles* in the blazing heat over terrain that would be hard on a mountain goat. I let you do that for the sake of a damn camera that could have been replaced for practically nothing. And you say that it's not important!"

"I couldn't have replaced that camera for any amount of money," she defended. "You were entirely right not to take Garcia up on his offer of the horse." She ran her hand distractedly through her hair. "I don't know why you're upset. I made it, didn't I? You even complimented me on my endurance!"

"That's because I'm such a blind fool that I can't see an inch in front of my face!" His angry glance raked her face and form. "Just look at you," he said disgustedly. "A strong wind would blow you away. Yet you've been jumping out of balloons, sleeping on the ground, and hiking miles through the hills. Don't you have any sense at all?"

"If you recall, I didn't have much choice in the matter," Kelly retorted angrily, her green eyes blazing. "What was I supposed to do? I guess the traditional feminine thing would have been to pull the Camille bit and lean on your big, wonderful chauvinistic strength!" She stood up, her hands clenching into fists. "Well, that's not me, damn it! If that's what you want, then you don't want Kelly McKenna." She whirled and stomped angrily toward the bedroom.

She had gone only a few paces when Nick's hand grasped her shoulder and turned her to face him. His thoughtful gaze took in her flushed face and quivering lips. "But I do want Kelly McKenna," he said quietly. "I want her very much."

"Then why were you so angry?" she asked throatily, blinking away the tears. "You made me feel like some sort of criminal."

He took her in his arms and cradled her tenderly, his hand gently massaging the tension from the muscles of her back. "Because you scared the hell out of me," he said softly. "What you went through in the last few days would have put a strain on the endurance of a marine commando, sweetheart. If I'd known you weren't well, I could have spared you a hell of a lot more than I did." His hands began to stroke the muscles of her neck, and she could feel her anger and tension ebbing away. "You could have ended up back in the hospital thanks to that blasted stubbornness."

"I told you that I'm well now," she said wearily, resting her head on his chest. "Why won't you believe me?"

"Because you're a gutsy broad with more courage than sense." His voice was soft. "I want you to promise to let me know from now on if there's anything—and I mean *anything*—wrong with you. Okay?"

"Okay," she said huskily, feeling a bursting happiness that he should care. "I guess I've just been on my own so long that it never occurred to me to discuss my problems with anyone."

He pushed her a little away from him to look down into her face. "I guess neither one of us is used to having our space infringed upon," he said quietly. "And God knows our relationship to date has been so turbulent that it would be a bloody miracle if you did feel close enough to me to give me your confidence." He frowned. "We started at the wrong end, Kelly. Our physical chemistry is so strong that I didn't have the patience to go through the rituals that usually precede a serious affair. All I could think of was getting you into bed."

Kelly opened her mouth to speak, but he stopped her with a gentle hand across her mouth. "No, listen to me," he said slowly. "I've been thinking about these weeks that we'll be here, cooling our heels and waiting for the paperwork to be cleared away. I think we should use that time to go back and start over." He grinned suddenly, the twinkle in his eyes banishing all sternness. "You're a fantastic lover, Goldilocks," he said. "I'm curious to test your potential as a friend."

Kelly could feel the delight that his words engendered in her expanding in her breast like the blossoming petals of a flower. "I'd like very much to become your friend, Nick," she said huskily, over the lump in her throat. Then because she felt that she was going to weep if the atmosphere wasn't lightened, she added teasingly, "Providing said friendship doesn't preclude me from continuing as your lover. Now that I've learned the knack, I wouldn't want to lose it for lack of practice."

He chuckled and hugged her affectionately. "No chance of that, sweetheart. Now that I've had you, I couldn't do without you if I tried. It's been less than thirty-six hours, and I'm already suffering withdrawal symptoms."

His lips closed tenderly on hers. But it had been too long for both of them, and they were overwhelmed with passion. Suddenly they were melting together in a fever of hunger. When their lips parted, they were both breathing heavily and clinging to each other with an almost desperate urgency.

Nick buried his lips in her soft hair. "Oh, Lord, you taste good," he said thickly. "So good."

"So do you," Kelly said faintly, her lips moving caressingly along his neck and throat. "I don't think that I could do without you now, either."

"Good." He slipped an arm about her waist and turned her gently toward the master bedroom. "Because I think that you just may be ready for that demonstration on Bedouin love practices that I mentioned."

"That gown is definitely a success," Nick said, cocking his head to consider Kelly objectively. "You look like a sexy wood nymph tonight."

Kelly looked down at the elegant empire-waisted chiffon gown she was wearing. It was lovely, she thought, and the color emphasized her eyes. "Can wood nymphs be sexy?" Kelly asked skeptically. Then, as Nick, with a distinctly wicked gleam in his eyes, opened his mouth to reply, she went on hurriedly. "Never mind. I should have known better than to give you a lead like that. I'm sure you could quote reams of erotic mythology tales to prove your point."

Nick leaned back in his chair and grimaced. "Pity. Properly told, mythology can be very arousing. I was trying to lure you out of this disco den and back to the hotel. Aren't you tired of this cacophony?"

"No, I'm not," Kelly replied firmly, looking at the gyrating figures on the dance floor. "I'm trying to recognize some of the beautiful people that Mr. Sykes told us use this nightclub as a meeting place." She wrinkled her nose at him. "I realize that it may not interest you, but we peasants find the jet set fascinating."

"You're right," he said slowly, his eyes traveling lingeringly over her eager face and smooth, bare shoulders. "You're the only beautiful person that I'm interested in at the moment." He reached out across the damask-covered table and took her hand in his.

Kelly felt a glow of happiness flow through her as she looked down at their clasped hands. She felt beautiful tonight, she thought, but it had more to do with the look in Nick's eyes than the gorgeous green chiffon gown that she was wearing, though the right clothes definitely did help a woman's morale. In the two weeks they had been in Acapulco, Nick had taken her to every major sightseeing point in the resort town, from the ancient Fort San Diego that had stood over the harbor since the seventeenth century to the famous cliff divers who could be seen with horrifying clarity from the El Mirador Hotel.

She remembered how fascinated she had been as she had watched the graceful beauty of those men as they dove from the cliffs, defying the jagged rocks below to enter the water. She hadn't even been aware that Nick had been watching her face and not the divers until he leaned forward and spoke in her ear.

"I should never have brought you here, Goldilocks. Now, if I don't watch you like a hawk, you'll be down here tomorrow wanting to try your luck on the cliffs."

Laughing, she had looked up at him, thinking that he was joking. But she had been surprised to see a curious tightness about his mouth. He really did think that she was addicted to danger if he thought that she would try to dive off those cliffs. Her eyes went back to the young Mexican diver who was readying himself for the dive. Still, it must be fantastically exhilarating, she thought wistfully. "No, I can barely swim a stroke," she said, as the diver launched himself in a spectacular swan dive. "We moved around so much when I was a child that I never had a chance to learn properly."

"Thank God," Nick said fervently, relief washing over his face. "I was planning on coming down here tomorrow and issuing a blanket bribe to all the divers to keep them from taking you on as a pupil."

She giggled. "You've got to be kidding." Then, as she noticed the grim expression on his face, she said indignantly. "It must take years of training to learn to dive like that."

"Exactly." Nick's blue eyes were hard. "So you're to stay away from those cliffs. Understand?"

She had no intention of trying a dive that would be pure suicide, but Nick's arbitrary arrogance pricked at her independence. She lowered her eyes and said thoughtfully, "I'll have to consider it. It must be wildly thrilling to fly through the air like a bird and then experience the shock as you hit the cold sea below."

Nick's eyes narrowed on her face, and he studied her demure expression and the flicker of mischief in her green eyes thoughtfully. "Okay," he said abruptly. "But you'll not go alone. If you're so set on taking the dive, then we'll both do it. I'll see about hiring a diver tomorrow to give us instructions." He leaned back in his chair and grinned. "Since I'm paying the tab, I'm sure that you won't mind my taking the first dive."

Kelly's eyes flew to his face in swift alarm. "You're joking," she said uncertainly. Nick's hard expression gave no clue to his thoughts, and she had a sinking sensation that he meant it. "Do you know anything about diving?"

"Not much," Nick admitted cheerfully. "But then I didn't know anything about hot air ballooning until I tried it."

"If you recall, your attempt at that couldn't exactly be termed a success," she said, biting her lip worriedly.

"But you've made it sound so appealing, I find I can't wait to try it. What do we care if there's a little danger involved?"

"A little danger! Just a slight miscalculation would send you crashing into those jagged rocks instead of the sea." She felt almost ill at the thought of Nick's body hurtling through space with those murderous rocks waiting below. Oh, God, why hadn't she let it alone? She knew Nick's fondness for taking chances, and now there was every probability that she was going to have to stand and watch him risk his life on those damn cliffs.

"I've changed my mind," she said desperately. "I don't want to do it."

"You're sure?" Nick inquired, arching a dark brow quizzically. "What about the thrill of flying through the air like a bird?"

She shrugged carelessly. "It can't be all that exciting." She heard Nick's low chuckle and glanced at him suspiciously. His dark face was alight with satisfaction. "Did you set me up, Nick O'Brien?" she demanded indignantly. "Would you have been at that cliff-top tomorrow?"

"You'll never really be sure, will you, Kelly?" he said teasingly. Then his eyes darkened, and the amusement gradually faded from his face. "The only thing that you can be certain of is that from now on before you leap from *any* cliff, either literally or figuratively, you'll have to stand by and watch me do it first."

A wave of emotion, a bewildering mixture of happiness and panic, washed over her. How maddeningly clever of him to realize the silken bonds that his words placed on her. She knew that she'd never be able to watch Nick deliberately put himself in danger without trying to stop him. "You're a wily devil, Nick O'Brien! But has it occurred to you that that particular sword cuts both ways?"

"Oh, yes, I realized that. And I can't say that I like my actions being curbed any more than you do. Keeping that pretty neck of yours in one piece is posing more problems than I ever dreamed possible." He took her hand in his. "While we're together I guess we'll just have to get our thrills in the bedroom."

She looked away and tried to ignore the sharp pain that the transient note of that last comment had given her. "I guess we will," she said huskily.

She forced her thoughts back to the present. As she looked down at their clasped hands on the nightclub table and listened idly to the blaring disco music, she could not imagine an existence without Nick O'Brien at her side. The thrills hadn't all been in the bedroom, she thought contentedly. Besides the really breathtaking sexual affinity that existed between them, they struck sparks off of each other mentally as well. Nick probably could have annihilated her in any real discussion, but there was not a hint of patronage in his manner as he listened to her opinions and arguments. She also found that they shared both a sense of the ridiculous and a restless curiosity. Add it all together and the sum was encouraging enough to fill her with hope for the future. She had been practically walking on air for the past two weeks, and Nick had seemed as contented as she. His desire for her had seemed to grow and not diminish, and they spent a shocking amount of time in each other's arms exploring that most fiery and primitive of pleasures. But she was almost sure that he also found the less turbulent aspects of their relationship as satisfying as she did. She couldn't have imagined the tenderness that she sometimes detected in his face in even their most platonic moments.

"You're very quiet suddenly. Are you sure you don't want to go back to the hotel?" Nick asked gently. "If you're tired, we can come back tomorrow evening to see your 'beautiful people.'"

She shook her head. "No, I'm not tired," she said, looking around the dimly lit room disappointedly. "But I certainly don't see anyone who looks particularly exotic here." She pouted. "You've been known to run with that pack occasionally. Don't you recognize anyone?"

Nick shook his head. "Sorry, Kelly. Maybe nobody told them that this was supposed to be their favorite hangout. Why are you so interested in the Acapulco jet set?"

"I thought I'd get a few photos to send to Mac to prove that I'm not just sitting on my duff while we're waiting for our papers to come through," she said, her gaze still searching the room. "He wasn't too pleased about the delay when I talked to him on the phone last week. He said it was taking longer to get out of Mexico than if it was an iron curtain country."

"Didn't you tell him about the marriage complication?" Nick asked casually.

Kelly shook her head. "I would never hear the end of it. Mac is certain that I'm trouble prone anyway. There's no sense giving him additional ammunition to play with. No, I'll just try to get him some filler shots to pacify him. That is if I—" She suddenly broke off, her hand tightening on Nick's. She bent forward to ask excitedly, "Nick, look at that booth in the far right corner of the room on the other side of the dance floor. Those two men are very familiar. Do you know who they are?"

Nick glanced casually at the two well-dressed men in the booth that she'd indicated, and his face abruptly became totally expressionless. "They look just like any other well-to-do businessmen," he said. "They're not the jet-setter types that you're looking for, Kelly."

Her gaze narrowed suspiciously. "Are you sure you don't know who they are, Nick? I'm sure that I've seen both of them somewhere before. If I recognize them, then someone with a memory like yours surely would."

"I said that they weren't who you were looking for," he said impatiently, frowning. "Now drop it, Kelly."

She bristled in annoyance. "You're being awfully evasive, Nick. Why won't you—"

"Nick, *querido*, how wonderful to see you again." The woman's voice was deep and sultry, and Kelly didn't even have to turn around to see the woman who possessed it to know that her appearance would match it. She had heard that voice before, and quite recently at that.

"Hello, Maria, this is a surprise," Nick said coolly, looking over Kelly's shoulder at the woman who had greeted him. "What brings you to Acapulco?"

Maria drifted forward in a cloud of very potent Chanel No. 5 to lean over and kiss Nick lingeringly on the lips. "I'm visiting the Gomezes at their villa. Don't you remember that I said I might come down in a week or so, *querido*?" She smiled at him, patently ignoring Kelly. "Acapulco is usually most amusing in this season, but I've been quite bored—until tonight."

Nick had said that she was obvious, Kelly thought gloomily, and she couldn't conceive of a more blatant invitation than the one she was offering Nick at the moment. She was practically melting all over him, Kelly noticed disgustedly, and he certainly wasn't resisting. Well, who would want to resist a dark, lush beauty like Maria Dominguez? In a white lamé halter gown slashed almost to her waist in front and baring her back to her very curvaceous derriere, she looked more like a Hollywood sex goddess than the wife of a government official. Even her face was sexy, with those sloe black eyes and a pouty mouth framed by that long, glossy, dark mane.

Nick at last pulled his attention away and turned to Kelly. 'Kelly, I'd like you to meet an old friend, Maria Dominguez," he said, his lips twitching with amusement. "This is Kelly McKenna, Maria."

"Delighted," Maria said lifelessly, not taking her gaze off O'Brien. Good Lord, the woman was practically eating him up with those hungry, dark eyes. "Are you going to dance with me, Nick?"

Obvious, indeed. Nick didn't appear to resent being pursued, however. He grinned tolerantly and said, "It would hardly be courteous to leave Kelly alone at the table, Maria."

"Don't mind me," Kelly muttered crossly, her envious eyes assessing the portion of Maria Dominguez's anatomy that Nick had said he favored. She wasn't about to sit here and watch the Latin woman attempt to seduce Nick. She jumped to her feet and grabbed her purse from the table. "I was just going to powder my nose anyway." She flounced off in the general direction of the restroom. She distinctly heard Nick swearing under his breath, but she wasn't about to return and be forced to watch Nick's former mistress trying to work her sensual magic on him. She stayed in the restroom for a good fifteen minutes. She carefully redid her makeup, ran a comb through her hair, then spent the time sitting impatiently with her hands folded, waiting for the minutes to pass and fuming about the aggressive boldness of a certain South American woman.

The sight that met her eyes when she finally left

the powder room didn't improve her temper. It took only one swift glance to determine that there was no one at the table and another to spot Nick and Maria on the dance floor. He obviously hadn't seen fit to get rid of her, she thought moodily, watching Nick's amused smile as he looked down into the woman's vivacious face. She stood at the edge of the dance floor debating whether she should just leave the club and grab a taxi back to the hotel or meekly return to the table and wait for Nick to finish amusing himself with the luscious Maria. It didn't take her long to come to a decision.

She was turning to make her way through the crowd toward the front entrance when she caught sight of the two businessmen whom she and Nick had been discussing before his former mistress had arrived. She stopped, a puzzled frown clouding her face. Despite what Nick had said, she was sure she'd seen both men somewhere before. Now that she was only a few yards from the booth where they were sitting, she was even more convinced that she was right. Particularly the large bearded one in the gray pinstriped suit. That hawk nose and bushy black brows were characteristics that could scarcely be forgotten, once seen. Well, she couldn't stand around undecided, gawking at them all evening. She'd just have to take a few shots of them and study the prints later.

She reached into her purse and brought out her Leica before tucking the purse under her arm and winding her way determinedly toward the men in the booth. She paused a few yards away and lifted the camera from where it had been hidden in the flowing panels of her chiffon skirt and focused it swiftly.

"Say cheese, gentlemen," she said clearly, then shot the picture as they both looked up startled. "Thank you," she caroled cheerfully and walked swiftly away.

She had gone only a few paces when two burly men in dark suits suddenly erupted from a nearby table and stepped in front of her menacingly. Kelly's eyes widened in alarm as she took in the truly intimidating bulk of the men and the fierce scowls on their faces. As an experienced journalist, she was quite familiar with the *genus* bodyguard and these specimens were easily recognizable. She felt a thrill of satisfaction surge through her as she realized that she must have hit pay dirt after all. Unknowns didn't hire professional bodyguards to protect them. Now all she had to do was get the film safely out of the reach of these goons and find out just who she'd unearthed.

That task might be more difficult than it sounded, she thought warily, as the enormous baldheaded guard circled behind her, while the smaller but equally husky man stepped toward her aggressively. He held out his hand commandingly. *"La cámara, por favor."*

"No way, buster," she said sweetly, smiling at him serenely. "Haven't you ever heard of the freedom of the press?"

It seemed that neither of them had, for she felt the baldheaded man's arms suddenly envelop her from behind. She kicked back at his shin with all her force, and he gave an agonized grunt and instinctively loosened his hold. She took the offensive. Turning with lightning swiftness, she grabbed his arm, stepping into a judo move she'd been taught and flipped him to the floor. But she'd had to put her bag and camera on a table to make the throw and the smaller man was scrambling eagerly to get the Leica. She kicked out at his face as he reached for the camera, and he fell backward with a surprised bellow of pain.

Kelly snatched up her bag and camera and took off at a dead run across the dance floor, dodging recklessly among the startled couples. She had almost reached the ring of tables encircling the dance floor when she felt herself literally scooped off her feet from behind and held kicking and struggling at least two feet from the floor. It must be the bald-headed one, Kelly thought frantically, the smaller man wasn't big enough to hold her dangling like a rag doll. Darn it, she couldn't get any leverage to do any real damage, and in another minute the other one would be here to grab the camera while she was being held helpless. She drew back her elbow to try a blow to her captor's solar plexus, when she heard him give a low grunt that was more like a sigh. His arms relaxed with startling suddenness, releasing her. Unprepared for the move, she stumbled but regained her balance in an instant.

"Come on," Nick said sharply, his hand grasping her elbow. "Let's get the hell out of here before you get us both murdered." He was almost running, and after one hurried glance at his grim expression, she decided to ask questions later and keep pace with him.

She couldn't resist one fleeting look behind her, however, and she almost stopped in her tracks when she saw her baldheaded captor lying unconscious on the dance floor, surrounded by a crowd of shocked and chattering people. She caught a brief glimpse of the hawk-nosed object of her photo moving rapidly toward them across the room, and then they were out of the club and running toward Nick's rented black Ferrari. By the time the bearded man erupted explosively from the entrance of the disco club, followed closely by his short, burly bodyguard, Nick and Kelly were already pulling out of the parking lot.

Eight

Kelly looked back over her shoulder and waved cheerfully at the two furious men who were glaring at them. Then she turned around and settled herself comfortably in the plush gray velvet bucket seat. "They appeared to be a trifle annoyed with me, didn't they?" she asked lightly. "Do you think they'll try to follow us by car?"

"How the hell should I know?" Nick said, between his teeth. His eyes were fixed straight ahead as he negotiated the traffic, and his knuckles as he grasped the steering wheel were white with tension. "It depends on how badly they want that film in your camera."

Kelly affectionately caressed the Leica on her lap. "They seemed to want it very badly, indeed." She chuckled. "By the way, what on earth did you do to that baldheaded joker to put him out of commission so efficiently?"

"I applied pressure on the cortex nerve in his neck,"

130

he said tersely. "A light pressure causes unconsciousness, more can kill a man."

The coldness of the statement shook Kelly for a minute, but she rallied swiftly. "You do have the most interesting facts stored in that computer brain of yours," she said teasingly. She was on a curious high, her blood pumping that exhilarating adrenalin, but it seemed that Nick was not sharing her excitement. She stole a glance sidewise at his grim, set expression and repressed a slight shiver. No, Nick was definitely upset, and that was completely out of character. She frowned in puzzlement. She knew enough about Nick's background to know that under normal circumstances he would have thoroughly enjoyed this brouhaha. Why was he so uptight tonight? "That must be a very handy thing to know. You must teach it to me sometime."

"It wouldn't have done you much good tonight," he said bitterly. "Your friend who looked like a sumo wrestler could have broken your back like a matchstick if he'd chosen. Or hadn't that occurred to you?"

It hadn't, as a matter of fact, and she was not about to dwell on it now that the danger was past. "He did rather look like a sumo wrestler, didn't he?" she asked. "My first impression was the Incredible Hulk, but your description comes much closer." Her eyes darkened thoughtfully. "They certainly got upset over one little photograph. I'll have to have this developed as soon as I get back to the hotel and see if I can find out who they are."

Nick swore and shot her a sidewise glance that was definitely menacing. "Are you telling me you deliberately caused that riot back there, and you didn't even know whose picture you were taking?"

"I knew that they were VIPs," she defended. "I just didn't know who they were." She frowned crossly. "And I didn't deliberately start the trouble at the disco. It just happened. How did I know that they were going to react so violently to having their picture taken?"

" 'It just happened,' " he mimicked caustically. "Disasters like that seem to happen to you with suspicious regularity. You rush in where angels fear to tread, and then you're surprised when a land mine blows up under your feet!"

"I was just doing my job," she said hotly. "I'm a reporter, damn it! I know very well there's a story behind that beard if I can just tag a name to it."

"The name is Sheikh Abdul Khadir," Nick said tersely, "and the other man is Colonel Ramon Cordero."

Kelly's eyes widened in surprise. "You knew all the time!" she accused indignantly. "Why didn't you tell me?"

"Because I knew you'd do exactly what you did," he growled. "Once you'd sniffed a story of that potential, you wouldn't have given up no matter how dangerous the ramifications were. Khadir is OPEC's money man and principal troubleshooter. He was bound to have a few toughs on hand for protection and persuasion."

"And who is Ramon Cordero?" Kelly asked.

"A very influential figure in the Mexican military establishment, as well as a man who has his fingers in quite a few choice government pies."

"Oil reserves," Kelly said flatly. "And some very lucrative wheeling and dealing for Colonel Cordero." She bit her lip in concentration. "Just how powerful is the military faction in Mexico?"

"Very. And growing stronger all the time. In an economic chaos, a military junta headed by Ramon Cordero might just topple the government."

"Oh, Lord!" Kelly whispered delightedly, her eyes glowing with excitement. "I can't wait to get this picture to Mac. He'll be over the moon!"

"And you'll be about six feet under ground," Nick

said grimly. "You might mention that when you tell him what a brilliant investigative reporter you are."

"You're exaggerating," she protested. "There wasn't that—"

"Shut up, damn it!" he interrupted harshly. He drew a deep breath and said slowly between his teeth, "In case you haven't noticed, I'm a little perturbed with you, Kelly. It wouldn't even be too far off the mark to say that I'm furious. So if you want to get back to the hotel in one piece, I suggest that you refrain from opening your mouth and making any more idiotic statements."

"Idiotic! Nothing I've said or done tonight has been idiotic, and it's—"

"Kelly!" The name was not loudly spoken, but it contained enough sheer menace to cut off her speech.

"Oh, very well." She gave him a disgruntled glance. "But don't think that I don't intend to continue this discussion once we get back to the suite."

He gave her a look so cold that it sent shivers down her spine. "I'm looking forward to it," he said with dangerous softness.

There was a frigid silence between them until the front door of the suite closed behind them. Nick flicked on the overhead light and strode directly to the bar at the far end of the room. He poured himself a double brandy and consumed half of it in one swallow before glancing at Kelly standing in the center of the room.

"I won't ask you if you want a drink," he said as he came around the bar and half sat, half leaned against a white velvet, padded bar stool. "You've had quite an intoxicating night already, haven't you, Kelly?"

"You're being completely ridiculous. I refuse to stand here like a naughty child being chastised by a stern parent for merely doing my job." Her hand tightened around the camera she was still clutching in her hand. "If you'll excuse me, I'll take this film out and get it ready to forward to Mac."

Nick's lips tightened, his face grim. "I won't excuse you," he said flatly, then took another swallow of his brandy. "You're not going anywhere until we have this out." He frowned impatiently. "You needn't worry about your precious film. You nearly paid too high a price for it for me to let anything happen to it. We'll run it to the airport tomorrow and send it out special counter-to-counter into your editor's eager hands. Now, put that camera away and sit down."

Kelly thought for a moment of defying him, but there was something intimidating about Nick at the moment. She moved with insolent leisureliness to the white velvet couch and placed the Leica on an end table before dropping down onto the couch. She waved her hand in mocking obeisance. "As my lord commands."

"Very amusing. You'll forgive me if I found your performance less than entertaining tonight. I never did care for black comedy."

Kelly slipped out of her emerald sandals and tucked her feet beneath her. "Aren't you overreacting? After all, there was no real damage done. I took a picture, and there was a little awkwardness, but no one was hurt. You've been involved in far worse scrapes in your career, Nick."

"I'm not five-foot-nothing, and I don't weigh in at less than half of my chosen antagonist," he said sharply. "Why in the hell didn't you just give them the film? Did it ever occur to you that Arab men don't take kindly to being physically humiliated by a woman? I saw that baldheaded bruiser's face, and he was killing mad. You were lucky he didn't take you apart with his bare hands."

"I had no idea that he was an Arab, and I was doing pretty well until he grabbed me from behind," Kelly bristled indignantly. "You needn't treat me like I'm some sort of fragile flower just because you helped me out of a spot. If you hadn't been there, I'd have gotten out of it on my own. I've been taking care of myself for quite a few years without your intervention, Nick O'Brien!"

"It's a wonder that you've managed to survive so long if tonight was an example of your damn suicidal impulsiveness." His expression was stormy as he finished his drink in one swallow and crashed the empty glass on the bar. "Do you know how I felt when I saw you up against those two goons and knew that either one of them could put you in the hospital before I could reach you through the crowd?"

"I wouldn't have thought you'd have noticed. If I remember, you appeared to be very occupied with Señora Dominguez before any of the rhubarb started. How did you manage to tear yourself away from the sexy señora?"

"You know that I don't give a damn about Maria. I only used her to try to distract your attention from Khadir."

"That's scarcely complimentary to either of us," Kelly retorted fiercely, ignoring the surge of relief that rippled through her at the realization that Nick had not been as dazzled by his former mistress as she had believed. "Your little South American chili pepper may not mind your attempting to manipulate her, but I certainly do. I'll run my life and my career to suit myself, and I'll be damned if I'll tolerate your interference. What if I tried to tell you how to do your job? You can bet that you'd toss my advice back into my face so fast that it would make my head swim."

"That's different. My job doesn't demand that I take on a roomful of toughs just to get a story."

"Granted," Kelly replied with acid sweetness. "You usually do that just for entertainment. At least I had a logical reason for what I did!"

"Logical! You don't know the meaning of the word." His blue eyes were blazing in his angry face. "You almost got yourself killed for a damn picture. Well, I'm tired of worrying what hell you're going to get into next."

"Who asked you to worry about me?" Kelly cried. "I told you that I could take care of myself!"

Nick straightened slowly, and his face was hard and set as granite. "Then I'll leave you to do just that," he said bitterly, as he strode swiftly to the door. "Because God knows I wish that I'd never let you into my apartment that afternoon in San Francisco!" He slammed the door behind him with explosive violence.

Kelly stared at the door for almost a minute before she could fully comprehend that he had actually left her. "Oh, damn," she whispered, feeling the tears brim over and run helplessly down her cheeks. "Damn you, Nick O'Brien. I hate people who walk away from a fight!"

And damn her own unruly tongue, she thought miserably, as she stood up and padded slowly toward the master bedroom. Why couldn't she have played it cool for once in her life and tried a little feminine persuasion instead of displaying her usual belligerent independence? What if Nick was gone for good? She wandered disconsolately into the gold-and cream-tiled bathroom, discarding her clothes carelessly as she went. She pulled on her shower cap, stepped into the shower stall, and turned on the warm spray. Annoying tears still continued to run down her face despite her efforts to stop them.

She'd certainly picked a fine time for making Nick angry, with that sultry nymphomaniac ready to leap on him. What if he was on his way to her right now? He knew where she was staying, she'd made quite sure of that. Oh, Lord, she wouldn't be able to stand it if Nick had left her for good. Damn Nick O'Brien for having this power to tear her emotions to pieces. It wasn't fair that anyone should be able to wreck another person's life just by slamming a door and walking away.

She stepped out of the shower, pulled off her shower cap, reached for a voluminous white bath towel, and proceeded to dry off with automatic thoroughness. She draped the towel around her carelessly and wandered back into the bedroom, her bare feet sinking into the plush cream carpet. She carefully folded back the gold satin spread on the bed and slipped between the sheets, tossing the towel carelessly on the floor. The silk sheets were cold and clammy against her bare flesh and only served to increase her feeling of being bereft.

She had been perfectly right to stand up to Nick, she assured herself staunchly. He had been unreasonable, chauvinistic, and completely unfair. She didn't care a tinker's damn if he was with that big-bosomed bitch. It certainly didn't matter to her if he never came back. It was totally illogical, then, that after all these firm self-admonitions, she proceeded to cry herself to sleep.

The brush of his lips was petal soft against the throbbing hollow of her throat. Kelly arched her throat instinctively as those caressing lips moved lightly up her throat to her cheek and then hovered over her parted lips, nibbling at the lower one with incredible gentleness. She was aware of a delicious sense of well-being that only half pierced the veil of sleep that enfolded her.

"Nick?" She sighed contentedly, not opening her eyes.

"Uh-huh," he growled softly against her lips, still toying with them with that magical tenderness, playfully tugging at their pouting fullness with his teeth. "Open your mouth, love. I want to taste your sweet honey."

He didn't wait for her languid compliance. His

marauding tongue entered and explored with leisurely enjoyment. There was no hurry, no urgency, and only a hint of underlying hunger as he garnered the sweetness he'd demanded.

Kelly slid her arms over his bare shoulders to curve around his neck, vaguely aware that he was sitting on the bed beside her and bending over her, his arms cradling her. He felt so strong, so warm, so wonderfully *here*, she thought. She had a dim, frightening memory of a loneliness so terrible that she pushed the thought away. It must have been a dream. For here was Nick holding her in his arms and locking out all the loneliness and insecurity in the world.

But it hadn't been a dream, she recalled. "You weren't fair, Nick," she muttered drowsily, pressing her lips lovingly to the hard plane of his cheek. "And you walked out on me," she recalled with languid indignation.

"Shh," he crooned, his hands pushing the sheet from her shoulders to bare the silky hollows to his lips. "I know, love. But you nearly scared me out of my mind when I saw that tough roughing you up." His lips brushed against her still wet lashes. "You've been crying," he said wonderingly. "God, I'm sorry, sweetheart. I know it wasn't really your fault this time."

"This time!" Kelly opened her eyes, sleep suddenly banished. Nick was naked to the waist, and his golden, sinewed beauty robbed her of a little of her annoyance.

"Well, you couldn't expect a total surrender," he said, kissing the tip of her nose. "We're far too much alike for you to think that I'd let you claim a victory of that magnitude. You'd never let me live it down."

Her lips curved in a reluctant smile. "Beast," she charged, trying to ignore the caressing movement of his hands on her bare shoulders. "I'd never be so ungenerous." Her face clouded stormily. "And I'd never walk out on you in the middle of an argument! Where did you go?"

"I had to get away and cool off," he said, nibbling at her earlobe. "I just drove around for a while and then took a long walk on the beach." His tongue darted with mischievous suddenness into her ear, sending a convulsive shiver through her. "Then I decided to buy myself back into your good graces by giving you a present."

"A present!" Kelly exclaimed, darting an incredulous look at the clock on the bedside table. "It's almost four o'clock in the morning. Where would you be able to buy a present at this hour?"

"Like the boy scouts, I'm always prepared," he said smugly. "As it happened, I already had a bribe on hand in the hotel safe for just such a delicate situation."

"Do you always keep gifts on hand to pacify your women friends?" Kelly angrily pushed him away.

He shook his head. "It was never necessary before," he said breezily. "My strong, virile body and devastating charm were always reward enough before you came on the scene, Goldilocks. Now, close your eyes."

She obediently did so. She felt herself lifted into a sitting position on the bed and pillows banked behind her to support her. He was gone for a brief moment, and then the mattress sank beneath his weight as he sat down beside her and took her in his arms. He kissed her lingeringly, pressing her bare breasts to his muscled chest until she was melting like warm butter from the explosive friction they were generating.

When their lips finally parted, Kelly was breathless and clinging to him with glowing passion. "Wow!" she said softly, nestling closer to him. "Is that my present? I'm beginning to believe that those other women may have been right about your fatal fascination, Nick."

He chuckled. "It's nice to be appreciated, but as it

happens that wasn't your reward. It was mine. You looked so sexy sitting there all cuddly and bare breasted that I decided to accept your gratitude in advance." Kelly felt something slip over her head and then the touch of cool metal on her throat. She started to open her eyes, but he put his hand over them swiftly. "Keep your eyes shut, woman. I haven't finished yet." Her right wrist was lifted from the sheet, and she felt again that cool metal embrace. Without dropping her wrist, he quickly slipped a ring on the third finger of her right hand. "Okay, you can look now."

He was still holding her hand in his, so the first thing she saw was the jade and gold ring with its dainty leaf design.

"My ring!" Kelly exclaimed, her expression stunned. "But, how?" She touched the ring with a loving finger. There could be no mistaking that distinctive design. She had last seen this ring on the plump little finger of Carmen Rodriguez in the village of Matzalea.

"As soon as we arrived at the hotel and Sykes arranged for a cash advance, I contacted Father Miguel and arranged for him to buy it back from Carmen." He lifted her hand and kissed the palm lingeringly. "I had an idea that it meant more to you than you admitted."

"Yes," she said huskily, looking down at the ring through a veil of tears. "My father gave it to me for my sixteenth birthday. He said that green was a lucky color and I should have a bit of it on my finger as well as in my eyes. I've always considered it my lucky piece."

Nick's face clouded. "And you traded it for baths and meals for us," he growled disgustedly. "Do you think I'd have let you do it if I'd known?"

"No," she said and gave him an impudent grin. "That's why I didn't tell you." Her gaze had now shifted from her finger to her wrist, and her eyes widened in surprised delight. "It's beautiful," she said softly, staring at the exquisite slender gold and jade bracelet. "It exactly matches my ring. You must have had it specially made."

He nodded. "The jewelers here in Acapulco are decent craftsmen, and they're fairly speedy." He lightly touched the necklace at her throat. "There are some matching earrings in my jacket pocket. Would you like me to get them?"

She shook her head, trying to swallow over the lump in her throat. She bent her head to brush her lips lovingly across the back of his hand.

"No. I can't accept them," she said huskily. "It's all too much, Nick." What an incredibly touching thing for him to do, she thought. She felt as if every atom of her heart and mind were flowing out to him, and suddenly she loved him so much that it hurt almost unbearably.

"Of course you can," Nick said arrogantly. "The jewelers won't take them back, and I don't know any other woman whose eyes would match them." His blue eyes twinkled. "Of course, I suppose I could give them to Cantina Carmen."

Her hand clutched at the bracelet in instinctive possession. "You will not," she said sharply. "I'll find a way to buy it from you. I probably can't pay the entire amount at once, but I'll arrange something."

Nick's eyes were dancing as he assured her solemnly, "I didn't think that galloping independence of yours would allow you to accept my humble offering without a fight, so I've resigned myself to letting you pay for them."

"You have?" she asked suspiciously. "That's very sensible of you."

He nodded cheerfully. "I thought so. Now all we have to do is set a price. What will you offer me?"

Kelly felt an odd melting tenderness as she looked into that mocking, reckless face. What would she offer him? All her love, a lifetime of loyalty and commitment, companionship, passion. "What do you want?" she asked huskily.

Nick's hand left her throat and wandered up to tangle in her blond curls. His eyes had darkened, and the amusement had been replaced by taut hunger. "That's a loaded question if I ever heard one," he said thickly, as his lips lowered slowly until they were only a fraction of an inch away from her own. "But it's one that I intend to answer both explicitly and frequently tonight." His tongue was lightly outlining the pouting fullness of her lower lip. "But for the moment, I can think of only one thing I really want, Goldilocks. Do you realize that I've never made love to a woman wearing only a jade necklace?"

Kelly swiftly lowered her lashes to veil the sudden pain that shot through her. Well, what had she expected from him? Nick had no use for the other gifts she could bring to their relationship. He had shown her tonight just how ephemeral their affair was going to be. Someday soon he would slam out of a door in anger, or worse still, close it quietly in weary boredom and walk away for good. This heady passion was the only emotion that he wanted to invoke in her. "No, I never realized that, Nick," she said lightly. "Is it one of your fantasies?"

"Well, now that you mention it," it *is* one of the tamer ones. We'll go into the more erotic varieties later. Will you pay my price, sweetheart?"

Suddenly her arms went around him, and she pulled him to her with an urgency bordering on desperation. Burying her head in his shoulder, she said, "Yes, I'll pay your price, Nick." There was a painful lump in her throat. She was paying a higher price than he dreamed possible, she thought miserably.

It was almost unbearable knowing that this was all she would ever have of Nick. Perhaps it was stupidly old-fashioned of her to be unable to accept the physical magic Nick offered in such abundance and be content. But she wanted more, damn it! She wanted Nick to love her as she loved him, and she knew now that she wasn't going to be able to stand the agony of staying with Nick and waiting for him to tire of her.

"Hey! I appreciate your enthusiasm, but your nails are digging into my back, kitten," Nick complained. He gently loosened her arms from about his shoulders and pushed her away, looking down at her. "Is there something wrong, love?"

She shook her head, still not looking at him. "No, everything's fine," she said huskily. "What could possibly be wrong? I guess if I want to satisfy that fantasy of yours, I'd better get undressed." She was conscious of the concern in his narrowed eyes as he watched her slowly unfasten the bracelet and take off her ring. With some effort, she painted a bright smile on her face as she handed him the jewelry. "Keep these for me, will you? I don't seem to have any pockets."

"That's not precisely accurate," he said, his eyes on her face. "I don't think you're being honest with me, Kelly, but I want you too much right now to care." He shoved the bracelet and ring carelessly into a pants pocket and drew her tenderly back into his embrace. "You're sure that you want this, Goldilocks?"

"Yes, I'm sure," she said quietly. She wanted him in that moment with a hot intensity that was tinged with desperation. "I want you to make love to me, Nick."

"Good," he said, reaching behind her and removing the pillow she was propped against and tossing it aside. "Because I don't think I could stop now regardless of how you felt." He lay her back on the bed. "God, I'm aching for you, Kelly."

His lips covered hers with a hunger that was almost bruisingly frantic. He settled himself beside her on the bed and impatiently ripped the sheet from her naked body. His hands were hotly eager as they ran over her soft curves. "You're going to have to stop me if I hurt you," he said. "I'm so wild for you I might not notice." His lips were covering her face with a multitude of hot kisses. "When I was walking on the beach tonight, I was thinking about this," he said, as his lips nibbled at one nipple. "How you tasted and felt." His lips moved to the other breast. "How you fit me." His teeth pulled playfully at the hard tip, causing her to moan sharply as a jolt of desire rippled through her. "I was half afraid you wouldn't be here when I got back to the apartment. I was all set to start scouring Acapulco for you. Then I walked into the bedroom and saw you curled up like a woeful baby." He gave her breast a final kiss and rolled away from her.

He stood up, his hands working hurriedly at his belt while he looked down at her, with an expression of glazed intensity. "When I was in the Orient, I spent a little time at a certain house in Hong Kong studying the nuances and techniques of physical lovemaking." He threw the belt carelessly aside and began to strip off his slacks. "My very capable tutor assured me that there were ways of making love to a woman that would bring her to such a pitch of ecstasy that it would spoil her for experiences of lesser intensity." His lips curved in a rueful smile. "I thought she was crazy. Who the hell would want to sexually enslave any woman so completely that she was able to respond only to you? It would curtail my freedom even more than hers."

He was totally nude now. Slipping back into the bed, he gathered her into his arms. His face was strangely grave as he looked down at her, his hand rubbing the softness of her belly with a sensuous rhythm that caused a shudder of desire to wrack her body. "I've changed my mind," he said thickly. "I don't want you to be able to let another man touch you without wishing he were me." His knee nudged her legs apart, and he gently eased his body down on hers. "I don't care about your freedom or mine." The smile on his face was savagely sensual as he ended softly, "Let's see if I learned my lessons well, sweetheart."

She thought later, as she lay in his arms in an agony of release, that if he'd learned his lessons any better, she would have gone out of her mind. She had always known that Nick was a fantastic lover, but tonight he had seemed to be driven with an obsession to bring her to a dazzling peak of desire that culminated in a hurricane of sensation. Even as she lay in his arms with her breath coming in gasps and her heartbeat gradually steadying, she could still feel her flesh burning and aching with remembrance of Nick's fiery manipulations. She didn't know whether Nick's little Chinese madam would prove correct at this point, but she did know that she had just experienced the ultimate in sensual pleasure.

Nick tucked her head in its accustomed place in the hollow of his shoulder and kissed her lightly on the temple. "Go to sleep," he ordered gently, as he pulled the sheet over both of them. "We're both exhausted. It's been a hell of a night in a variety of ways, Goldilocks."

Kelly nodded drowsily, only half hearing the words as she nestled closer to him. Then she felt Nick's fingers at her nape, and she asked sleepily, "What are you doing?"

His soft laugh barely stirred the curls at her temple. "I'm finishing with your disrobing, love. The realization of my fantasy was infinitely satisfying in every way, but this blasted necklace scratches." He drew the jade necklace away from her throat and dropped it on the floor beside the bed. "Besides, I want to be close to you tonight." His lips brushed her closed lids tenderly. "I don't want even a breath between us."

Kelly felt her throat tighten with tears even as she instinctively nestled closer into the security of his embrace. No matter how close they were physically, there was a gulf as wide as an ocean between them, she thought sadly. As beautiful as these shining moments were, they couldn't sustain her through the pain that would follow. She knew that now. But it was so good to be held in this tender travesty of love that it was almost enough. Tomorrow she would clear her mind and heart of this pitiful self-deception. Tomorrow she would force herself to make the decision that she knew must be made. Tonight she would sleep in his arms and pretend that he loved her as she loved him.

Nine

When she awoke, the noon sun was streaming through the closed satin draperies, flooding the bedroom with a mellow golden haze. The first thing that pierced her consciousness was the fact that she was alone in the king-sized bed and the second was the presence of a tray with coffee and juice on it on the bedside table. She sat up dazedly and brushed the tousled curls from her eyes just as Nick strolled in from the adjoining bath. He looked disgustingly handsome and wide awake in the black suede pants and aqua shirt. His dark hair was gleaming from the shower.

"It's about time you woke up, woman." Nick grinned as he plopped down on the bed beside her and gave her a quick kiss. "I've been banging around this room like a herd of elephants hoping I could wake you before I yielded to temptation and crawled back in bed with you." He tousled her blond curls affectionately before reaching for the juice on the bedside table. "I ordered some coffee and juice for you. I thought we'd wait until I got back from my appointment for a big meal. We could go down to the beach and have a picnic lunch. Would you like that?"

"Very much," she said absently, as she took the glass from him. "Where are you going? What appointment?"

"While you were sleeping like Rip Van Winkle this morning, I received a phone call from that lawyer Sykes put me in touch with. He says that he has everything about wrapped up as far as his investigation regarding our marriage is concerned, but there are a few minor points that he wants clarified. I told him that I'd drop into his office this afternoon. It shouldn't take more than an hour or two." He reached for the carafe of coffee on the bedside table and poured a cup for her.

"If he's completed his work, then we should be able to leave Mexico soon," Kelly said slowly, trying to hide the sinking feeling of disappointment she felt. Had she really secretly hoped to talk herself out of the decision that she'd made the night before? she wondered sadly. It seemed that even without her initiating the break, their affair was drawing rapidly to its own conclusion.

"We'll see," Nick said. He pulled the sheet down to her waist and kissed each nipple with casual affection before he pulled her into his arms and nuzzled her throat like a friendly puppy. "Will you be here when I get back or down at the pool?"

"I'm not sure," Kelly said huskily, her arms tightening around him with a trace of desperation in their grasp.

"It had better be down at the pool if you want to have any lunch today." He reluctantly released her and got slowly to his feet. "Either that or be fitted with a chastity belt while I'm gone."

"I'll keep that in mind," she whispered, her gaze running lovingly over the striking planes of his face.

He bent down and gave her a swift, hard kiss that promised much for the coming afternoon, then turned and strolled toward the door. He paused and turned back to her, a frown creasing his forehead. "I forgot about that blasted film of Khadir and Cordero. Would you like for me to drop it off at the airport on my way?"

She shook her head. "I have more time than you. I'll do it myself," she said quietly. "It's my responsibility."

He shook his head. "Why did I assume you'd accept my help graciously?" he asked. "You certainly never have before. I'll leave the matter entirely in your capable, liberated little hands then." With a mocking wave he was gone.

Kelly gazed blindly down at her coffee cup, feeling her throat tighten uncontrollably at that last remark. It took such a short time for an intimacy such as theirs to breed private little jokes and habits. How many times in the last weeks had Nick teased her about that almost belligerent independence? If only he knew. Lord! Independence? How terribly painful it was going to be to break the bonds that linked her to him.

Yet break them she must. She had never had any masochistic tendencies, and a lingering end to her affair with Nick would be too excruciating for her to bear. Perhaps if last night's argument had never happened, if she had not experienced the tearing sense of loss when Nick had so violently departed, she might have continued to fool herself that she could stay with him until he finally tired of her. Though Nick was displaying no signs that his passion for her was waning, she knew now that the awareness that his obsession for her was purely physical was the thorn among the roses that would eventually pierce her to the heart.

God, how mawkishly melodramatic she was becoming, she thought impatiently. Just because she'd been stupid enough to fall in love with the wrong man was no reason for her turning herself into a soap opera heroine. She was too strong to let one maddening, blue-eyed man destroy her like this. She was a survivor, and she'd be damned if she would end up as one of Nick O'Brien's heartbroken discards. She put her untouched cup of coffee down on the tray on the bedside table and threw the cover aside decisively.

Twenty minutes later she had finished showering and was dressed in elegant cream-colored pants and a matching bloused tunic top. It was a coolly sophisticated outfit, and she had chosen it to reinforce her own need for self-determination and control. The ploy wasn't meeting with any marked degree of success, however, she thought morosely, as she slipped on brown alligator high heels and ran a comb quickly through her curls. The only way she was maintaining even the semblance of control was by deliberately blocking out all thoughts of Nick and keeping her mind on the details that needed to be considered in her departure. As she deftly applied a touch of lipstick and a little mascara, she considered the difficulties she might encounter as a result of her decision to leave Nick. It must be today and before Nick returned if she was to leave at all. She knew her resolution would waver like a candle flame in the wind if she had to face Nick with her decision.

She frowned as she remembered that she still had no proof of citizenship, which she would need for crossing the border. The plane fare would be no problem. She'd had Mac wire her an advance the day after she'd arrived in Acapulco. But cutting the red tape with immigration required more clout than she possessed. Her face brightened as she recalled that Mac Devlin, though now anchored to a desk, still had contacts all over the world from the time he was a foreign correspondent. Surely if she appealed to him, he could pull a few diplomatic strings for her. She strode briskly to the extension phone on the bedside table and quickly placed a long-distance call to San Francisco.

It was all incredibly easy, once she'd gotten through to Mac and voiced her request. With his usual gruff incisiveness, he told her to jump into a cab and head for the airport. He would have her cleared with the Mexican officials by the time she reached the ticket counter. Kelly sat for a stunned moment before she finally managed to ask blankly, "But if it was that simple, why didn't you pull me out of here before?"

"Why the hell should I?" Mac replied tersely in his gravelly voice. "You needed a vacation after that bout in the hospital, and it was the only way I could get you to take one. If I'd told you how easy it was to come back home, you'd have been in my office two days later nagging me to pay off that bet and send you off to Timbuktu to interview the resident headhunters."

"You even griped at me for not being able to break the red tape and get back to work!" she said indignantly.

"Do you think I'm stupid?" Mac demanded. "What better way was there to assure that you'd stay there than to hassle you to come back? If I'd told you to stay down there in the sun and put on a few pounds, you'd have turned wetback to get across the border!"

"Very clever. Where did you get your diploma in psychology, Dr. Devlin?"

"The school of hard knocks." He sighed wearily, and she could almost see him run his hand through his gray-streaked hair. "Don't get on your high horse, Kelly. You know you would have reacted in exactly that fashion if I'd played it straight, and you needed the rest, damn it. How are you feeling now?"

"Fine," she retorted, still fuming. "And why are you letting me out of exile now?"

"Because I've found a way to keep my word and still manage to keep you out of trouble until you're back to full strength. How would you like to go to Antarctica with an oil exploration team?"

"It sounds like just what I need after two weeks in sunny Acapulco," Kelly said gloomily.

"Well, it's so cold that it's almost completely sterile down there," Mac said cheerfully. "Even the microorganisms can't survive at that temperature. You sure as hell won't come down with malaria again."

"That's comforting. When do I leave for this germ-free utopia?"

"Eight days. The oil company is sailing from Seattle next Saturday at three in the afternoon. That should give you some time to shop for your long underwear and do some background research on the project. Okay?"

She made a face at the phone. "As if I have a choice, Mac Devlin. You've probably already subleased my apartment and given my desk at the office to somebody else."

"You were never here long enough to make good use of it anyway. Now get going to that airport while I phone a couple of good buddies and collect a few favors. Call me from the airport and tell me what plane you're arriving on." Without waiting for a reply, he hung up the phone.

There was a grudging smile on Kelly's face as she replaced the receiver and rose to her feet. Despite her indignation at Mac's deft manipulation of her, she had to admit that it gave her a little inner glow to realize that it had been affection that had motivated his actions. If she was going to get through the next lonely months without running back to Nick and begging him to resume their relationship, she was going to need all the support she could muster—although Mac's assignment in the frozen wastelands of Antarctica should efficiently prevent her from indulging in that insanity for quite a while.

She quickly checked her brown alligator shoulder bag for cash and makeup, then slipped her camera with its precious film into the bag. She would leave all the clothes that Nick had bought her since they had arrived in Acapulco. He'd never allow her to pay for them, and she wanted no more reminders than she had now of those bittersweet weeks. She used all her willpower to resist taking a final nostalgic tour of farewell of the suite and walked briskly through the front door and closed it firmly behind her.

"You look like hell," Mac said bluntly, after giving her a quick hug of greeting at the San Francisco Airport. He took her elbow and briskly propelled her through the usual late afternoon crowd toward the short-term parking lot. "I thought you said you were feeling fine."

"I am fine," Kelly said firmly. "You know that I can never sleep on jets." She darted a rueful look at him as she half skipped to keep up with his long-legged stride. "You're looking disgustingly fit, Mac."

In his early fifties, Mac Devlin always looked devastatingly attractive with his gray-streaked hair and piercing gray eyes. His bold, craggy features were more interesting than handsome, but she knew that women of all ages found him very magnetic. "You've got a deeper tan than I have."

"Marcy and I have been spending the past few weekends at the beach house."

Marcy was Mac's wife of nearly twenty years and the reason why other women didn't stand a chance with Devlin. Marcy was one of the most beautiful redheads Kelly had ever seen and was as honest and warm as she was lovely. She balanced a thriving career as an actress with her equally successful marriage and was at present the shining light of the San Francisco repertory stage.

"She's not in a play right now?" Kelly asked, as she slipped into the passenger seat of Mac's red Toyota.

He shook his head. "She's in rehearsal for a revival of *All My Sons* at the moment. It opens next week." He slammed her door and sprinted around to the driver's seat. As he put the car in gear and backed out of the parking space, he continued, "I called her and told her that you were arriving this afternoon, and she wants to see you before you leave for Seattle. I'm taking you straight to the beach house for the weekend."

"I'll have to stop by my apartment and pick up some clothes," Kelly said, as she watched admiringly as he deftly maneuvered the Toyota into the rush hour traffic. "I didn't bring any luggage from Mexico."

"I noticed." He cast a curious look at her. "I was being my usual discreet, urbane self in tactfully ignoring both the urgency of your call and the fact that you must have spent two weeks in Mexico totally nude." He grinned. "I hope you appreciate that, Kelly."

Kelly's mouth twisted wryly. "I never noticed you being so shy before."

Mac shrugged and changed the subject. "I'm not about to fight my way through this traffic to get to your apartment. Marcy keeps a closet full of clothes at the cottage. You can wear something of hers."

Kelly shrugged. "Whatever you say," she said wearily, closing her eyes and leaning back on the headrest. It didn't seem worthwhile to mention the fact that Marcy was five foot nine and voluptuous.

"You're very docile all of a sudden," Mac remarked gruffly. "You're sure that you're okay?"

"Yes, I'm sure," she said, opening her eyes and forcing a bright smile. "But you might want to stop at the office and have this processed before you take off for the weekend." She reached into her shoulder bag and withdrew the roll of film and put it on the seat between them.

"What is it?" Mac asked, glancing down at it. "I told you there was nothing urgent about that feature story about O'Brien. You can write the story up this weekend. We'll probably wait to use it in an issue next month."

"It's not for the O'Brien story. It's a shot of Shiek Khadir in an intimate tête-à-tête with Ramon Cordero at a nightclub in Acapulco." She shot a sly glance at his astounded face. "Of course, if you think that story can wait until next month, too, we'll just wait until Monday to have it processed."

"Not likely," Mac said, his gray eyes gleaming with excitement. "Has anyone else got the story?"

She shook her head. "Exclusive," she said quietly and watched Mac's grin widen delightedly.

"Dynamite. We'll drop the film off first and then drive down to the beach house and you can write the story tonight. I'll have someone pick it up tomorrow morning and rush it into this week's issue before there's a leak."

"So much for my leisurely weekend with Marcy. May I have dinner first, Simon Legree?"

"I'll consider it," he said, his gray eyes twinkling. "It's only one evening. You'll have the whole weekend to gossip with Marcy."

"Your generosity is staggering. Have you forgotten you also wanted me to finish the O'Brien story this weekend?"

"Well, there's always Sunday," Mac said, as he pulled into the underground parking garage of the skyscraper that housed the offices of *World Weekly*. "What are you complaining about? You've just come back from a two-week vacation!"

It was over an hour later when they resumed their journey and almost twilight by the time they reached Mac's beach house.

"Marcy's not here yet," Devlin observed, as he

parked the car beside the gray, weathered, two-story cedar structure with white-shuttered windows. Though not large, the house had a graceful serenity. A sundeck ran along the entire length of the front, overlooking the blue waters of the Pacific. "The rehearsal must be running late. They've been having problems with that ingenue who's playing Ann." As he got out of the car, he looked at the horizon and frowned. "There's a fog rolling in. I hope to hell that she's already started."

Kelly could understand his concern. At this time of year, the fog came in with a frightening speed and blanketed the coast with a thick mist that could be very dangerous to motorists.

"Marcy wouldn't be foolish enough to drive if there was any real problem," Kelly said comfortingly. "She likes life too much to take any chances."

"Not like some people I know," Mac said, giving her a meaningful sidewise glance. "With a prize like me as a husband, she'd be insane to risk suicide on that freeway."

Kelly grinned. "She probably arranged to arrive late on purpose so that you'd have to start dinner. And don't think you're going to get me to do it. I'm a guest."

Mac scowled. "Women's work," he snorted disgustedly, as he unlocked the front door of the house.

"Bull," Kelly said succinctly, smiling sweetly. "*This* woman's work tonight is pounding out the Khadir story on that ancient Smith-Corona you own. I fully intend to be waited on hand and foot while I'm doing it." She breezed past him into the small foyer of the cottage and headed for the stairs. "I assume that I have the same guest room?"

"Yes," Mac said gloomily, as he watched her trip lightly up the stairs. "I hope you know that your next assignment is going to be a travel feature on the delights of Death Valley."

She made a face at him. "Well, it's bound to be a change from Antarctica!"

It was quite a while later when she finally left the guest room. She had spent a good deal of that period just struggling to retain the bright mask she'd assumed for Mac's benefit. She was finding it incredibly difficult acting her normal self when all she wanted to do was throw herself on the bed and wail like a banshee. But she forced herself to take a shower, and then she tried to disguise with makeup a few of the signs of her emotional upheaval that Mac had picked up so quickly.

In her weary and depressed state, she found it exasperating to search through Marcy's closet for something to wear for dinner. Absolutely nothing fit. She had almost given up in despair when she ran across a full burgundy skirt that she knew would have to do. Thank heavens Marcy's waist was as pencil slim as her own, she thought. The hem probably hit fashionably about Marcy's knees, but it almost touched her own ankles and could have passed as an evening skirt. There was no way that she could fit into one of Marcy's blouses, so she had to be satisfied once again with donning her own tunic top. By tightening the matching cream sash at her waist and opening the buttons at the throat to show just a hint of cleavage, it made a very tolerable mate for the velvet skirt. She shrugged indifferently as she looked at the rather bizarre gypsyish figure in the mirror. What difference did it make, anyway? There would be only Mac and Marcy at dinner, and then she would be banished to the typewriter to pound out the Khadir story. Well, the outfit did look rather wild and carelessly gay; perhaps it would add to the cool, uncaring facade she wanted to project tonight. Her sophisticated alligator pumps would have looked ridiculous with the ensemble, so she deliberately left her small feet bare.

She finally left the guest room and danced lightly downstairs, a sunny smile painted on her face. Her smile faded, however, as her gaze fell on the bank of windows that faced the staircase. Generally, even in the evening the view was spectacular from those windows, offering enchanting glimpses of silver sand and white, curling foam on the midnight darkness of the surf. Tonight there was nothing to be seen but the thick gray mist that pushed against the glass as if it were trying to get in. She had not heard the phone ring since she had gone upstairs. Was Marcy still out in this pea soup of a fog?

"Well, I'm glad you finally deigned to honor me with your presence," Mac said as he came down the stairs behind her. He had changed into jeans and a white knit, short-sleeved T-shirt that looked fantastic with his deep tan. "I noticed that you waited until everything was done in the kitchen before you put in an appearance." His keen gray glance raked over her. "Are you planning on telling fortunes after dinner?"

Kelly ignored the flippancy, her expression anxious. "Mac, have you heard from Marcy? I didn't hear the phone ring." She shivered as her eyes went back to the windows. "It's really bad out there."

He nodded casually. "That it is," he agreed. At the bottom step he slipped a friendly arm around her waist. "But Marcy's not out in it, thank God." He grinned sheepishly. "I was worried, so I called the theater and caught her before she left. I told her to wait until the fog lifted and drive up in the morning." He turned her toward the spacious living-dining area. "I explained that she wouldn't get a chance to talk with you tonight anyway, since I'd be cracking the whip to keep you at the typewriter."

"Well, I'm glad she's not out in this mess even if I won't have her to intercede for me," Kelly said, allow-ing him to lead her to the dining area on the far side of the room.

"She must think I'm getting old," Mac complained. "She was amazingly complacent about my spending the night alone in a deserted beach house with a luscious little blond. She even told me not to work you too hard." He leered clowningly at Kelly. "I tried to blast her with a witty double entendre, but she just laughed at me." He sighed. "Yep, she must think I'm getting old."

Kelly shook her head and laughed as she slipped into a captain's chair cushioned in a cheerful beige and gold print. "She just believes that you know the gold from the dross by this time," she said firmly, as she shook out her napkin. "And that you have the good sense to realize that she's the real thing."

Mac's hard face softened. "Yes, I'd be something of a fool not to know that after twenty years with the woman," he said thoughtfully.

Kelly felt her throat tighten with emotion at the expression in Mac's eyes. God, what she would have given to have Nick look at her like that. But she wouldn't think of Nick, she thought desperately. Not tonight. Not until the pain diminished with the passing of time.

"What are you feeding me tonight?" she demanded, a bright smile on her face. "I absolutely refuse to work without adequate sustenance. Even galley slaves will revolt if pushed too far, you know."

"If I recall my history, galley slaves were almost never served steak and salad," Mac said, striding toward the kitchen. "Nor were they waited on quite meekly by their overseers."

Mac returned with a tray containing both steak platters and two wooden salad bowls. "I've just completed my last duties as your host," he growled, as he went around to his own place and shifted his own meal from the tray. "From now on I'm your boss, and your first job is the cleaning up. Cooking at least has a little dignity. I absolutely refuse the humiliation of showing up at the office Monday with dishpan hands."

"I guess I can manage to subdue my liberated spirit to indulge you in that, Mac. Especially since I know Marcy had a whiz of a dishwasher installed last summer."

"Brat," Mac accused, as he cut into his steak. "It's not the labor involved, it's the principle."

"My thought exactly," she said demurely, as she took her first bite of the steak. "But I'll be very tolerant and not give you a lecture on the chauvinistic tendencies you've been displaying of late, Mac."

"Very kind of you, I'm sure. Yes, it's definitely Death Valley for you next, Kelly."

Kelly smothered a smile and changed the subject by asking about the supplies she would need to take on her assignment in Antarctica. For the rest of the meal the conversation was light and impersonal, and by the time she had finished her steak and salad, Kelly was mentally congratulating herself that she had completely fooled Mac into believing that she was as cheerful as the proverbial lark. Nevertheless, she was grateful when the meal was over.

"That was quite a decent offering, Mac," she said, folding her napkin and putting it beside her platter. "Now, I'll act the obedient slavey and clean up these dishes. Then I'll get to work on my more legitimate duties."

Mac's gray eyes narrowed. "The dishes will wait," he said abruptly. "There's coffee brewed in the kitchen. Suppose you get it while I build a fire. We'll move over to the couch and relax a bit." His gaze was oddly searching. "You can tell me all about Acapulco."

Kelly could feel a sinking sensation in the pit of her stomach. She should have known she could never fool Mac. Besides being one of the most analytical minds in the business, he knew her too darned well. "A fire in June, Mac?" she asked lightly, moistening her lips nervously. "I really should get to work on that story." She rose to her feet. "I can tell you about Mexico any time."

"Go get the coffee, Kelly," Mac ordered curtly, as he pushed back his own chair and stood up. "This dense fog has made it chilly and cool enough to merit a fire, and I've always found a nice blaze is a great way to relax inhibitions and inspire confidences." His glance was razor sharp as he repeated softly, "Go get the coffee."

She knew Mac's obstinate determination too well to question that tone. "Oh, very well." She sighed and walked toward the kitchen. "Just one cup of coffee and then I go to work."

When she returned with the teak tray containing the carafe of coffee and two cups and saucers, Mac was sprawled lazily on the burgundy couch before the fire, his legs stretched before him and his gray head resting on its high, cushioned back.

He sat up straighter as Kelly put the tray on the gleaming maple coffee table, then dropped down beside him. But it wasn't until she had poured their coffee and offered him his cup that he looked up from his absent absorption with the flames. "Thanks, Kelly," he said. "Waiting on a man obviously comes easily to you. Perhaps you're not as liberated as you think."

"I'm every bit as liberated as I believe I am, Mac Devlin," Kelly said tartly. After taking a sip of her coffee, she leaned back in one corner of the couch. "But like all modern women, I try to do everything that I attempt with equal efficiency."

"I see," Mac said with mock solemnity. He looked down at his coffee cup. Then, softly, he said, "Tell me about Mexico, Kelly."

"What can I tell *you* about Mexico, Mac?" she asked. "You probably know more about it than I do.

Didn't you tell me you spent three years there as a foreign correspondent?"

He nodded, his lips tightening. "Okay, so don't tell me about Mexico," he said flatly. "Tell me about Nick O'Brien instead."

Kelly inhaled sharply at the sudden thrust of pain that went through her. Trust Mac to go for the jugular. She looked away nervously and took another sip of coffee. "I'd rather not," she said quietly. "You can read all about him when I finish the story." She smiled sadly. "I think the average reader will be positively enthralled by the dashing Mr. O'Brien. He's quite a colorful character."

"And were you positively enthralled by him, Kelly?" Mac probed gently, his eyes on her face. "Is that why you're running scared for the first time in your life?"

That brought her gaze flying back to his face. "I'm not running scared," she denied hotly. "I'm just trying to follow that wonderful advice you're always giving me about looking before I leap and the virtues of discretion."

"You've never paid any attention to my words of wisdom before. Why start now?"

"Perhaps I'm growing up at last," Kelly said, putting her cup and saucer carefully down on the coffee table in front of her. Her hands were annoyingly unsteady, and Mac's gaze was damnably perceptive. "Why this sudden interest in Nick O'Brien? You've never interfered in my personal life before, Mac."

"I've never had to watch you tear yourself apart over a man before. You've always flitted on the surface of your relationships in the past. Why do I feel that this time you're in way over your head?"

"You seem very well informed." Kelly moistened her dry lips with the tip of her tongue. "How did you know that Nick O'Brien was anything but a story to me?"

"I still have contacts in Mexico, remember? And no one can say that either one of you was trying to keep your association a secret. That's one of the reasons I didn't pull you out of Mexico sooner. I didn't want to be accused of spoiling love's young dream."

She closed her eyes against the bittersweet memories that flooded through her, then opened them. "That was a mistake, Mac. I wish that you'd made me come home at once." Her eyes were bright with unshed tears. "You're right, I was in over my head."

Mac crashed his cup down on the coffee table. "For God's sake, Kelly, you haven't any more sense than a babe in arms! Hell, you knew O'Brien's reputation even before you met the man. You knew he was a world-class chaser and had no more sexual morals than a tomcat, yet you fell into his bed like a ripe plum. What the hell were you thinking of?"

"I wasn't thinking at all," she said sadly. "I was feeling. I'm in love with him, Mac." The words were surprisingly hard to get out, but she felt an odd sense of relief once she'd uttered them. She was suddenly no longer so alone in her desolation.

"Then you're a bigger fool than I imagined possible. You can't expect a commitment from a man of O'Brien's stamp. Why on earth did you let yourself become involved?"

Her lips twisted bitterly. "Nick says I have a passion for no-win situations. Perhaps he's right. You certainly can't be in a more hopeless position than to be crazy about a man like Nick." She leaned her head wearily against the high back of the couch. "I knew that all along, but it didn't help. Nick can be downright irresistible once he puts his mind to it. I didn't stand a chance."

Mac frowned. "The man can't be all that devastating. You were probably a sitting duck for a man of his experience. You're sure that it's not just sex?"

"I'm sure," Kelly said quietly. "I wish to God it was that easy." She shook her head. "Though I'll be a long while getting over that particular hangover as well."

"I didn't think you'd be bowled over by a mere infatuation," Mac said, surveying her with a tenderness not unmixed with exasperation. "You do have *some* sense under that go-for-broke impulsiveness."

"Thanks heaps. I know I can always count on you for sympathy and understanding, Mac."

"You can, you know," Mac said soberly. His hand reached out to cover hers. He gave it a comforting squeeze before continuing with gruff gentleness. "You're the closest thing that Marcy and I have to a child of our own. Richard was my best friend, and over the years as we saw you growing up, I guess we got the feeling that you sort of belonged to us, too." He grinned wryly. "We may not be very experienced at this parental bit, but we'll always be there when you need us, Kelly."

Kelly felt her throat tighten with tears as her hand clutched at his as if he were a life preserver in the middle of an unfriendly sea. "Damn it, Mac, you're going to make me cry," she said shakily. "You've both been wonderful to me, and I love you very much." She drew a deep breath and tried to smile, but her lips were quivering uncontrollably.

"Now tell me about this bastard who caused you to send up that SOS. I suppose he dropped you for some other woman?"

She shook her head. "No," she whispered, looking down at their clasped hands gloomily.

He raised an eyebrow in surprise. "No? I thought surely that must be it considering O'Brien's reputation. What was it then? You quarreled constantly?"

She shook her head again. "No, we only quarreled once the entire time we were together. That only lasted for a few hours before we made up." She tried hard to banish the lump in her throat as she remembered exactly how they had made up that quarrel the night before.

Mac frowned impatiently. "Kelly, I have no intention of playing twenty questions with you. What did O'Brien do to you to send you scurrying home in a panic?"

"Nothing," Kelly protested tearfully. "You're speaking as if he's some kind of monster. No one could have been kinder or more generous to me than Nick."

Mac gave an explosive sigh and then with careful precision said, "If O'Brien's such a virtuous paragon, will you please tell me why you left the man, when it's obviously making you so hellishly miserable?"

"Because I knew it couldn't last, and I couldn't stay around and know he was growing tired of me," she said woefully. "You called him 'a world-class chaser.' Well that's not the only field he's world class in, Mac. How long do you think any woman could hold the interest of a man like Nick O'Brien? He's a miracle man!" The tears that had been brimming suddenly overflowed and ran down her cheeks.

"So you decided to run away and bury your head in the sand," Mac said slowly, his eyes fixed thoughtfully on her face. "I've never known you to run away from a challenge before, Kelly."

"There's a first time for everything, Mac," Kelly said despondently. "I find that I'm a miserable coward where my emotions are concerned. I'm not a changeable sort of a person, and I'd never have survived a break-up with Nick if I'd stayed with him any longer."

"Damn it, Kelly, it's not like you to be so humble," Mac said in disgust. "You've never been shy about recognizing your own value. How the hell do you know the man will tire of you? You're quite a person in your own right."

Kelly smiled sadly. "Thanks for trying, Mac, but you've forgotten one rather important fact. Nick doesn't love me. It's difficult to have confidence that any relationship will last without that ingredient."

"I guess that's true. But you don't have a chance in hell if you don't fight for what you want, Kelly."

Kelly's face was troubled as she carefully considered Mac's words. Was he right? Did she really have a chance of winning Nick's love? She felt a sudden surge of hope when she realized that she hadn't even given this most important challenge of her entire life her best shot. Why had she assumed that the situation was hopeless? Looking back she could see now that, from the moment she'd done the background research on him, she had let herself be intimidated by the mystique that surrounded him. But why should she take this defeatist attitude and run away before she'd waged even a token battle? Granted that Nick was unique in many ways, but she was pretty damn special herself. There was no reason on earth why Nick couldn't eventually be convinced that she was worth loving.

Her jade green eyes were suddenly blazing with hope as she cried eagerly, "Mac, you're fantastic. Why didn't I realize that—"

The rest of the sentence was drowned by a thunderous knocking at the front door that caused them both to jump. Mac released her hand and rose quickly to his feet. "Who the hell could that be?" he said, frowning. "It's certainly not a night for neighborly visits."

"Perhaps it's someone who has lost his way in this awful fog," Kelly suggested, as she watched Mac stride rapidly across the room. The thunderous knocking was repeated, this time with considerably more violence. Kelly made a face. "Whoever it is appears to be in a foul temper."

"Only a complete idiot would be wandering around outside on a night like this," Mac said. He threw open the door. His tall, muscular frame was blocking the doorway so that Kelly could not see their visitor, but she heard Mac's slightly impatient "Yes?"

Then she heard him mutter a surprised curse as

he was abruptly pushed aside and the visitor strode explosively into the house.

"Nick!" Kelly exclaimed, her eyes widening incredulously as she stared in openmouthed bewilderment at the stormy-faced man who was standing glowering furiously at her. "What are you doing here?"

Ten

"What the hell do you think I'm doing here?" Nick asked harshly, his eyes blazing blue fire at her across the room. "I've come to retrieve my runaway wife."

"Wife?" Mac's voice was as stunned as his face.

Kelly scarcely noticed. All her attention was focused on Nick O'Brien's dominant presence. That first surge of supreme joy and surprise had been swiftly superceded by a feeling of apprehension, for there could be no doubt that Nick was murderously angry. His face was taut and strained, his lips tight with the control he was exerting to suppress his fury. He was dressed in the same black suede pants and aqua shirt he had worn when he left the suite this morning. Was that only this morning? she wondered. It seemed a hundred years ago. He had rolled the sleeves of the shirt up to the elbow and unbuttoned the top buttons. He looked as tough and powerful as a stalking leopard.

Nick answered Mac's exclamation without removing his gaze from Kelly's shocked face. "Didn't she get around to telling you that we were married in Mexico, Devlin?" he asked between clenched teeth. "How very remiss of her. It must have slipped her mind."

"Kelly?" Mac asked bewilderedly, as he slowly closed the door.

"It wasn't important, Mac," she said absently, her eyes running over Nick's glossy ebony hair that was wet from the mist. "It probably wasn't even legal."

"Oh, but it was, my erring little spouse," Nick said. "If you think you can wriggle out of it through a technicality, you're very much mistaken. That marriage would withstand scrutiny in any court in the U.S., which gives me certain inalienable rights. One of which is to remove my wife from the love nest of a middle-aged Don Juan."

"Ouch. That hurt." Mac flinched. "You could at least have left out the middle-aged." There was a flicker of amusement in the depths of his gray eyes and a curiously satisfied expression on his face. "And I really don't think you should take Kelly out in this weather. It's not safe out there on the highways."

"Tell me about it," Nick retorted. "I've had to crawl blindly all the way from your office to this Eden by the sea, and it hasn't improved my temper. I'd be careful about offering any unsolicited advice at the moment, Devlin."

"Nick, don't speak to Mac like that," Kelly said indignantly, finally roused from her surprise to spring to Mac's defense. She jumped up and strode around the couch to face him belligerently. "Mac is not a Don Juan, and he's in the very prime of life."

"Thank you, Kelly, I needed that," Mac said dryly, leaning back against the door and crossing his arms over his chest. It was obvious he was enjoying watching the two of them. "But I don't think your husband is quite in the mood to appreciate your singing my praises at the moment. If you want to save my skin, I think you'd be wiser to let me keep a low profile."

"Don't be ridiculous," Kelly said crossly. "He can't just burst in here like a raging bull and insult my friends. I won't stand for it."

"Your boyfriend may be a trifle ungallant, but he has a hell of a lot more sense than you do," Nick said. "It would take very little to push me over the edge, Kelly. Now let's get out of here before I reorganize your boss's pretty features."

"Pretty!" Mac said, stung. He straightened up and glowered. "Now that's going a little too far, O'Brien. I'll reluctantly accept the aging, but I am *not* pretty."

"Don't you dare threaten Mac," Kelly said angrily, placing her hands on her hips and glaring at him defiantly. "Why should I go anywhere with an arrogant, mannerless dictator who hasn't even the courtesy to—Nick!"

His name was uttered in a furious shout as Nick covered the distance between them in two steps, grabbed her by the wrist, and turned and strode toward the door, pulling her forcibly behind him. "That did it," he said grimly. "You've just added the proverbial straw that broke the camel's back." He brushed Mac away from the door with a distinct lack of gentleness. "Good night, Devlin. I'm sorry to deprive you of your little playmate, but I have use for her services myself."

He opened the door, letting in a rush of cool gray mist, and dragged Kelly out the door onto the sundeck. They were immediately enveloped in the dense fog, and Kelly could feel the damp cedar planks of the porch steps under her bare feet as Nick pulled her relentlessly down the stairs. "Nick, this is crazy," she wailed, "We can't go wandering around in this fog. We can't even see where we're going." Then as they reached the bottom steps and her feet sank into the moist coolness of the sand, she added, "I haven't even got any shoes on!"

It evidently was the wrong thing to say, for Nick's hand tightened painfully about her wrist. "Yes, I noticed you'd made yourself very cozy," he growled furiously, his strides lengthening as he left the house behind. "You're damn lucky that I got there before you took off anything else, or I'd have killed the bastard."

"You're insane," she said breathlessly, trying to keep pace with him. "I told you that Mac was old enough to be my father."

"But you failed to tell me he was a Paul Newman look-alike or that it was your custom to spend weekends with him at his beach house," he said grimly. "I had to find that out for myself, didn't I, Kelly?"

"Paul Newman has blue eyes," she corrected. Now that she thought about it, Mac did look a little like Newman. "And he's been like a father to me. For goodness sake, he's married to Marcy Wilmot, the actress, and she's absolutely gorgeous. He wouldn't look twice at me."

"Then he's a complete ass," Nick retorted. "And somehow Devlin didn't impress me as being a fool." His pace didn't slow, and Kelly was now almost running to keep up with him.

"Nick, where the hell are we going?" Kelly cried in exasperation. "I can't see a yard in front of me. We just can't keep walking blindly like this."

"Why not? It's what I've been doing ever since I got back to that empty hotel suite this afternoon. Did it ever occur to you that it would be courteous to leave a note? I wasted nearly two hours looking for you before it occurred to me that you'd left me. I called the airport and checked departures and found that you'd boarded a plane for San Francisco. I was on the next flight out."

"I gather you had no trouble with immigration," Kelly said caustically. "Now isn't that peculiar?"

"No, I knew fifteen minutes after we arrived in Acapulco that we could get around the reentry requirements fairly easily. I'm surprised it took Devlin so long to find that out."

"You knew!" Kelly said incredulously. "Then why did you tell me it would take weeks to straighten out the red tape?"

"Because I wanted those weeks with you, damn it. I knew that I was going to need all the time I could beg, borrow, or steal."

All she could see was his broad shoulders as he pulled her along behind him, and she desperately wished that she'd seen his expression as he said those words that suddenly sent a ray of hope beaming through her. She abruptly dug her heels in the sand and pulled back with all her strength. Her abrupt resistance caught O'Brien off guard, and she pulled free with very little effort. She sat down on the sand and crossed her legs. "I'm not going one step further, trailing behind you like a bit of seaweed, Nick O'Brien," she announced clearly. "If you want to talk to me, we'll do it with a little dignity."

He scowled down at her for an undecided moment, then reluctantly dropped down on his knees facing her. "I guess this will do as well as anywhere. I just wanted to make sure that we wouldn't be interrupted."

"Interrupted?" Kelly stared at him as if he'd gone mad. They were on a deserted beach in the middle of fog so thick that she could barely make out his features, though they were only a few feet apart. Yet he spoke as if they were in a New York subway during the rush hour. Suddenly it struck her as hilariously funny, and what started as a surprised giggle, graduated to a whoop of laughter. "I think we're fairly safe from interruption here."

As she wiped her eyes on the back of her hand, she heard Nick's reluctant chuckle. "I guess you're right." There was a long moment of silence and then Nick said quietly, "God, I love to hear you laugh."

Kelly felt her heart leap in her breast as her eyes flew to the shadowy features before her. Surely his tone had held loving tenderness, but how could she be certain in the darkness? "I wish I could see your face," she whispered breathlessly.

"Your wish is my command, Goldilocks." Nick fumbled in his pocket, and suddenly the darkness was pierced by a narrow beam of light. Nick carefully planted the slender pocket flashlight upright in a mound of sand beside them then glanced at her, his brows arched inquiringly. "Better?"

She nodded. "I should have known you'd be prepared. Do you ever make a mistake, Nick?"

The light from the flashlight cast a halo of intimacy around the two of them, and she could now see the lines of weariness on O'Brien's face.

His tone was grim. "It seems that I've made a hell of a big one somewhere along the line. Why did you leave me, Kelly? I know that you were upset last night, but I thought we had that straightened out. Then I came back from that lawyer's office and found you'd left me without a word. If there was a problem, why couldn't you have stayed and talked it out with me, for God's sake?"

She shrugged, her gaze avoiding his. "I thought it best," she said evasively. "After I decided to go, there didn't seem any reason to drag it out any longer than necessary. Nothing you could have said would have changed my mind."

Anger flared briefly in the depths of his eyes. "You didn't give me the opportunity, did you? Because you knew damn well that I wouldn't let you go without a fight. You should have realized that I'd come after you."

"Why, Nick?" she asked softly, her eyes lifting to meet his with an eagerness that was impossible to hide. "Why did you come after me?"

"Because you belong to me, damn it," he said harshly, scowling at her fiercely. "You may not know it yet, but what we have is too good just to wash down the drain because you want to retain your blasted independence. There's no way I'm going to let you go flitting around the world free as a bird, when you've got me chained to you. You've got to learn that there are compromises in every relationship."

"I do?" Kelly asked dazedly, her eyes fixed in bewilderment on his face. Could this be the reckless, mocking Nick O'Brien, whom she doubted had ever made a compromise in his entire life, lecturing her with such sternness?

"You do," Nick said firmly. "I know you're afraid of making any permanent commitment to me, but you can't run away from it forever, Kelly. I'll try to keep the strings as loose as I can tolerate, until you get used to the idea." He grimaced. "As you've probably noticed, I'm not very patient, so I can't promise to extend that slack indefinitely."

"I see," Kelly said faintly, veiling her eyes with her lashes so that he wouldn't see the joy that was shining out of them. "That's very generous of you, Nick."

"No, it's not generous at all," he said curtly. "I'm going to stick as close as a shadow to you until you see things my way."

"That might be a little difficult. Mac's sending me on an assignment to Antarctica next week."

"Antarctica!" The exclamation was followed by a string of curses.

"Of course, I haven't bought my thermal underwear yet, so I just might be open to other offers." She looked up at him mischievously. "What alternative will you give me?"

He went suddenly still, and his eyes narrowed thoughtfully on her face. "Actually, I think I have an offer you can't refuse, sweetheart," he said slowly, as he shifted closer to where she sat in the sand. "Did you know that a team of Peruvian scientists has discovered a tablet with some fascinating hieroglyphics engraved on it in the mountains near the Nazca plain?" Not waiting for her to answer, he went on. "There are some features about the lettering that are completely foreign to anything ever found on earth."

"The Nazca plain," Kelly breathed, her eyes sparkling with sudden interest. "Wasn't that where they found the markings that they claim indicated a landing field for ancient astronauts?"

Nick nodded, grinning at the glowing eagerness illuminating her face. "I thought I'd get a team together and go down to see if I can find any trace of a connection between the two. If nothing else, the chance to study the tablet would make the trip worthwhile."

Kelly smiled at the excitement glinting in his aquamarine eyes. "The origin of man on this planet," she said softly. "The ultimate puzzle. How could you resist it?"

Nick's smile became coaxing. "And how can you resist it? The Amazon river is teeming with man-eating piranhas. There's the challenge of climbing the Andes, and I understand that some of the jungles of South America are still inhabited by tribes of headhunters. That should be enough to keep even you interested." He shifted closer so that they were only inches apart. He ended hoarsely, "As for the nights, I think that I can guarantee to keep you entertained."

"Only at night?" she pouted, gazing up at him in mock disappointment.

"That last offer is definitely negotiable," he assured her gravely. "You can be certain that you won't need thermal underwear in my bedroll, sweetheart. Will you come with me?"

"I don't see how I can turn you down," she said, an innocent expression on her face. "You make it sound so inviting. I do have one stipulation, however."

"Stipulation?" Nick asked warily.

Kelly nodded, looking away from him. "You've got to tell me that you love me," she said in a little rush.

"I love you."

She looked at him blankly. "Just like that?" she asked. "You were more eloquent describing the joys of the man-eating piranhas of the Amazon."

He frowned darkly. "What the hell do you want from me, Kelly? You've known that I've been absolutely insane about you since that first afternoon in my apartment. I've shown you in every way a man can that you're the most important thing in my life. Now you want the words so that you can officially add my scalp to your collection. Well, I gave them to you, but you can't expect me to embroider them prettily to your satisfaction."

Was that what he thought she was doing? She could see by his face that he did, and it stunned her that he would subdue his pride to the extent of giving her such a petty victory. She felt such a rush of love for him in that moment that she felt dizzy with it.

She threw herself into his arms with a suddenness that nearly knocked him from his knees to the ground. "Oh, Nick, I love you so much," she whispered, covering his face and throat with a hundred little frantic kisses, her arms holding him in a grip that almost robbed him of breath. "Why didn't you tell me? How was I supposed to know that I was anything but an amusement to you?"

Surprise held Nick frozen for a moment, then his arms enfolded her in swift possession. "Amusement!" he growled, torn between laughter and indignation. "You've robbed me of my freedom, put me through a hell of doubt and jealousy, you've even made me resort to trickery and subterfuge to keep you with me. I wouldn't say that I'd found you amusing by any stretch of the imagination." Then, as his hands wandered down and cupped her buttocks, he added,

"Though I have to admit you have definite entertainment value, Goldilocks."

She reached around and moved his hands firmly up to her waist. "This is supposed to be a tender declaration," she said sternly. "Pay attention."

"How about show and tell?" he suggested, nibbling at her earlobe. "I've always been better at that than rhetoric."

She shook her head and drew away, sitting back on her heels. "Later," she promised. "Now, I want to know all about the trickery and subterfuge that I've driven you to. I never realized that I was so irresistible, and it sounds positively fascinating."

He gazed at her thoughtfully for an instant before deciding to humor her. "Five minutes," he said. "I think I can manage to keep my hands off you for that long." He grinned at her sheepishly. "Though I should probably try to consolidate my position before I make my confession. I'm afraid I took shameless advantage of your ignorance of Spanish in Matzalea. Father Miguel had no real objection to our single status, once I'd explained the situation. The marriage was my idea. I wanted to have some means of binding you to me once we reached Acapulco, and it was the only lever that occurred to me. I had a fairly good idea that the marriage would prove valid."

Kelly was staring at him, her mouth agape. "The marriage was your idea," she repeated dazedly. "You wanted to marry me even then?"

He nodded, his expression amazingly loving. "I knew that I'd never want to let you go again when you told me you weren't afraid to jump with me from the balloon. Before that, I wanted that luscious little body with a stronger passion than I'd ever known before, and I knew you amused and intrigued me enormously." He grinned teasingly. "But how could I help falling in love with a girl who was willing to jump out of a hot air balloon without a parachute?"

"I did trust you," Kelly said softly, her eyes bright

with tenderness. "I knew that no matter how crazy and dangerous it seemed, that I'd be safe with you."

"You always will be," he said gently, his expression oddly grave. "Through piranha-swarming rivers and hot air balloons, through disco brawls and marauding bandits, in sickness and in health, as long as we both shall live."

"That's beautiful," Kelly said, her throat tight with tears. "I didn't understand a word of our wedding ceremony, but I'm sure that this is much better. I wish that I could think of something equally lovely to say to you."

"I'll settle for your promise to love me for the next fifty years or so," he said, "and never to leave me again. I went through hell this afternoon when I finally realized you'd gone." A puzzled frown clouded his face. "Damn it, if you loved me, why the hell did you run away from me?"

"Because I loved you so much," she said simply. Then, at his impatient frown, she explained, "It's not as illogical as it sounds. It's pretty scary falling in love with a superman. How did I know that you wouldn't get bored with me once the novelty wore off? You told me that once you'd found the key to a puzzle, the challenge was gone. I knew that for me it was going to be forever. I couldn't stand it meaning less to you."

He reached out, grasped her by the arms, and gave her a far from gentle shake. "I've spent my entire life fighting the prejudice that my IQ inspired in those around me," he said grimly. "Most people are either intimidated by me or harbor an active dislike because they imagine I look down on them like some sort of god from Olympus. Even my own father couldn't force himself to feel any affection for me. I'll be damned if I'll accept that kind of thickheaded thinking from you! What we've got together is too important to risk. We fit together in every way that could possibly matter. You're a woman of infinite variety, and I fully expect you still to be surprising me on our golden wedding anniversary. So if I *ever* hear you give me any of that crap about my getting bored with you, I'm warning you that I'll slap you silly!"

Kelly stared wide-eyed into his stormy face. "I'll remember that," she said faintly. Then recovering quickly, she gave him a breezy grin. "It was only a temporary aberration anyway. Once I'd thought about it, I realized what an incredibly lucky man you'd be to get a prize packet like me."

"Right," Nick agreed, pulling her into his arms. "Now that that's settled, let's get down to basics. Your five minutes are up." His lips covered hers in a kiss that was firm and sweet and dizzily persuasive. Not that persuasion was really necessary. It seemed like weeks, not hours, since Nick had made love to her, and she was as hungry for him as he was for her.

It was clear that Nick was very hungry indeed, as he tumbled her back in the sand, his body hardening in arousal as he pressed her into its grainy embrace. "I've been wanting you ever since I left you this morning." He deftly unbuttoned her tunic blouse and unfastened the front closure of her lacy bra. "I've been starved for the feel of you all day." Then his lips were working teasingly at one taut nipple while his thumb caressed the other.

Kelly could feel the familiar heat flow through her as she ran her fingers through his thick hair. "Nick, we can't," she protested weakly. "Not here."

Nick pressed his aroused loins to her and rubbed himself against her with a frank sensuality that caused her to give a little gasp. A jolt of pure desire shook her. "Can't you feel how I need you, love? I'm aching to have you hold me in that sweet, tight way you have." His teeth were nibbling and pulling her lower lip. "You said yourself that there was no chance of us being interrupted on a night like this."

Then his lips were covering hers. Kelly's arms slid slowly around his neck and pulled him even closer to her. Perhaps he was right. It seemed that they were alone on an alien planet, so complete was the privacy afforded by the thick blanket of mist that surrounded them. Strange that the abrasive sand beneath her body, instead of detracting from her arousal, actually increased it, as did the cool swirl of the fog and the sound of the surf hitting the shore somewhere nearby.

Nick was tearing at the buttons of his shirt, and at last his hard chest was pressed to her swollen, sensitive breasts. The hot surge of desire that shot through her banished her last inhibitions, and she clutched him to her with the same aching frustration that she felt in him.

"Love me, Nick," she whispered. "Please, love me."

His only answer was the harsh, ragged rise and fall of his breath as his hands moved over her in fevered, intimate caresses. Then his lips were exploring hers once again as he fumbled blindly at the tie at her waist.

At first she didn't notice it, so enraptured was she by the symphony being played with hands and lips. It was only after a wave washed over their supine bodies, almost completely engulfing them, that the cold shock of the water caused her to come abruptly to her senses.

"Hell's bells!" Nick roared, rolling off her and looking around the water-soaked sand with an expression of such outraged indignation that Kelly couldn't suppress a giggle. "What the hell's happening?" Another wave washed over them as if in answer, and Kelly started to laugh in earnest.

"I think the tide's coming in," she said, grinning and looking down at her waterlogged velvet skirt and sopping wet blouse. "And I always thought that beach love scene in *From Here to Eternity* was so romantic. What went wrong, Nick?"

He looked down at his own drenched clothing and shook his head, then chuckled in amusement. "God knows, sweetheart. Maybe next time we'll try it with a warmer surf and an appropriate musical score by John Williams." He got to his feet, grimacing as the water squished in his shoes, and reached down to pull her to her feet. He rescued the pocket flashlight, which was still working depite its dousing. "Much as I'd like to try it again, I think I'd better get you to some sort of shelter before you catch pneumonia." He swiftly fastened her bra and buttoned her tunic. "I have a rented car parked back at Devlin's house. We'll find a motel and continue this later."

"We'll do no such thing," Kelly said firmly, her chin lifting stubbornly. "We'll go back to the cottage, and you can apologize to Mac for all those terrible things you said to him. I'm not having the two favorite men in my life at odds with each other."

Nick scowled ferociously, and for a moment she thought he was going to refuse. Then, shrugging, he said gruffly, "Okay. I guess I was a little rough on him." He darted her a suspicious look. "You're sure that he has only paternal feelings toward you?"

"I'm sure," she said. "And if you're extremely charming to him, he might be persuaded to lend you something to change into while your clothes are drying."

"That won't be necessary. If he'll just lend us a bedroom, our own clothes will be dry before I let you out of bed anyway."

Nick's hand was linked with hers as they strolled almost leisurely up the beach. They were both cold and shivering, and there was absolutely no reason for them to be so wildly, ecstatically happy. No reason but the love that was flowing between them in an almost visible current of power. She felt as if they must be lighting up the misty darkness with their shining beacon of happiness.

"I hope we're going in the right direction," Nick said uneasily. "I was so angry that I didn't pay much attention to where we were heading after we left Devlin's house."

"I think we are," Kelly said, not really caring. She shot him an impish glance. "Don't tell me that you don't have a good sense of direction?"

"Lord, no," he admitted. "I've been known to get lost in a parking garage."

"Ah, a weakness at last," Kelly said teasingly. "I bet you're not Superman, after all."

"Only with you by my side, sweetheart," he said quietly, his hand tightening on hers. "Only with you in my arms."

THE EDITOR'S CORNER

What a New Year to look forward to from LOVESWEPT! Truly we have good news to help get your 1984 reading off to a superb start . . . and more! Our first good news is, of course, the three wonderful romances you can anticipate in our January list.

Much loved author Anne Reisser's last book was **BY LOVE BETRAYED,** published in September 1982. Now, as we mentioned last month, we're thrilled to announce that Anne's first new romance in all these long months is a LOVESWEPT! **LOVE, CATCH A WILD BIRD,** LOVESWEPT #28, is Anne Reisser writing at the top of her form. Bree Graeme is a captivating restless soul. Yet this young adventuress would have come home at a run had she only known what awaited her at her family's farm in the person of Cane Taylor. With spellbinding intensity Anne Reisser explores the very meaning of commitment between two people who desperately love each other. And, by the end of **LOVE, CATCH A WILD BIRD,** you will feel that Bree and Cane are close family to you, so well will you know their passions and their minds.

We're so proud of Iris Johansen and so pleased for her. With four books published, Iris has become a *very* popular romance author. And, isn't one of the most marvelous attributes of an author the growth she demonstrates with each new work she creates? Nowhere is that growth of a writer more obvious than in Iris's next LOVESWEPT, #29, **THE LADY AND THE UNICORN.**

(continued)

Janna, an elusive creature of exquisite grace, is unfettered by possessions or wealth. She collides with Rafe Santini, consummate materialist and hardened businessman, and forever changes his life. In **THE LADY AND THE UNICORN,** Iris has created an almost overwhelmingly evocative story, full of unforgettable imagery.

WINNER TAKE ALL, LOVESWEPT #30, by Nancy Holder is a book to relish—the one upmanship, the sheer fun when Wonder Woman meets Superman really makes for delicious reading! And Dick and Holly's consummation is as unique as their courtship—talk about turning a cold swimming pool into a hot tub! And what they manage to accomplish at his desk is nothing short of astonishing. Nancy Holder has published under a couple of pseudonyms since we read her first book, a Regency, about three years ago. We think that Nancy herself is a "winner to take all" in the romance sweepstakes! We're betting you'll agree and will look forward eagerly to this book . . . and all her future LOVESWEPT romances, too!

And now for our second piece of good news. We've been asked by many readers to increase the number of LOVESWEPT romances we publish each month. We've been thrilled with that outpouring of requests, but, of course, we couldn't and wouldn't publish more unless we were positive we could guarantee the consistent high quality of each book. That's what you've come to expect from LOVESWEPT, isn't it? That each romance we publish is a fine read? Well, with a delicious cache of love stories, we're delighted to tell you that we're confidently increasing our list. And, because Valentine's Day is our special holiday, we will begin publishing four romances each month with our February releases. I hope you'll be truly pleased to be able to look forward to one more excellent romance from LOVESWEPT each month starting in February!

May your New Year be filled with all the best things in life—the company of good friends and family, peace and prosperity, and, of course, love.

Warm wishes for 1984 from all of us at LOVESWEPT,

Carolyn Nichols

Carolyn Nichols
   Editor
LOVESWEPT
Bantam Books, Inc.
666 Fifth Avenue
New York, NY 10103

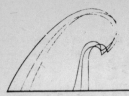

Love Stories you'll never forget by authors you'll always remember

SPECIAL
MONEY SAVING
OFFER

Now you can have an up-to-date listing of Bantam's hundreds of titles plus take advantage of our unique and exciting bonus book offer. A special offer which gives you the opportunity to purchase a Bantam book for only 50¢. Here's how!

By ordering any five books at the regular price per order, you can also choose any other single book in the catalog (up to a $4.95 value) for just 50¢. Some restrictions do apply, but for further details why not send for Bantam's illustrated Shop-At-Home Catalog today!

Just send us your name and address plus 50¢ to defray the postage and handling costs.